SUMMERS OF FRANCE
Amy Hayes Castleberry

Virginia Capes Publishing

2013

CHAPTER ONE

1990
Virginia Beach, Virginia

FRANCE DUG HER toes into the cool of the sand, arching her back and closing her eyes against the setting sun. Everything at the beach at that time of day was blue; the horizon that blurred where the ocean met the sky, the salty, sweet breezes that riffled the few remaining umbrellas clinging to the shoreline, ragged holdouts against the fading summer; the dunes and their clumped grasses that camouflaged the sandy boardwalk back to the cottage.

Squinting, she scanned the rooflines of the houses southward. She could see the silhouetted outlines of the large hotels in the distance, where the residential North End of the beach merged into the resort area.

It is still the same old beach, she thought to herself, although many of the weathered beach houses of her girlhood had been supplanted by gleaming new structures of steel and Hardiplank and man-made materials. Although change came slowly to this part of the world, she felt a sense of sadness when another familiar cottage was erased from the beach, the same sense of sadness as learning of an old friend's passing.

She smiled, picturing Daddy lining his little family up every summer with his list of chores to assist their cottage into another year of old age. He always maintained that it would keep them out of trouble. She sighed deeply at the memory. All the work in the world couldn't have accomplished that. So long ago.

Turning at the sound of a child shrieking, she watched as a family trundled down the sand toward the waves lapping at the shore.

"Would you mind taking our picture?" A blonde man with a bad sunburn grinned, holding a camera in the air, two sunburned children in tow.

Tourists, thought France. Probably renting one of the newer houses for the week.

"Not at all," she smiled, pulling herself to her feet. She took the camera, and waved everyone into position. How old were these parents? she wondered. Probably in their early thirties, she guessed.

"Everybody smile pretty," she ordered and snapped. She could see the future photograph in her mind, carefully placed in an album, tomorrow's memory.

A huge chocolate lab bumped her leg as she turned, almost knocking her down, his mahogany coat matted with wet sand.

"Steamer! No! Bad dog!" A skinny boy came running behind her, sprinting after the disobedient dog. "Sorry!" he called over his shoulder as he ran down the beach.

"Okay!" she called after them. She could see the dog joyfully destroying the few remaining encampments with happy abandon. She watched them until they were dots in the distance.

Heavily, she sank back onto her chair and settled in. She could feel the tenseness of the events of the day creep into her every muscle. She drew in her breath, willing every knot out of her neck. Today was Tally's wedding day. Five hours ago, her little dark-haired daughter had gotten married. What a sweet wedding it had been. She pictured Scott at the altar, tall and nervous in his Navy dress whites, trying so hard to look calm and controlled. She smiled, picturing the look on his face when Tally entered the little church on Steve's arm. Tally was a beautiful little bride, with her tawny skin and almond-shaped eyes.

She closed her eyes and could see Steve standing in Scott's place in that same spot, in his dress whites.

She remembered how startlingly blue his eyes were, his hair dark and his skin sun-browned after a summer at the beach, standing in the church of her summer childhood, with those mellowed walls of honeyed pine. He still looked good, she thought. He has aged very well. She could think this objectively while watching Steve guide little Tally to the front of the church where he placed her next to Scott before returning to his seat.

Twenty-two years ago, she thought in disbelief. Their wedding was so different from the wedding unfolding before her now. None of the months of planning that had gone into Tally's wedding had gone into hers. There just hadn't been enough time.

Her dress was hastily borrowed from her sister Martha, who had only just gotten married herself six months before. Mama summoned a few friends and a lot of family by telephone to attend. It was November, she remembered. A few remaining flowers from the Richmond farm festooned the rustic chapel. She could still feel the weight of Daddy's arm supporting her before the ceremony began as they stood at the entrance. Mama and Martha were fussing with her dress up until the last possible minute, coaxing the creamy ivory satin over the gentle swell of early pregnancy.

She noticed Tally's bouquet quivering ever so slightly during the vows and a rush of maternal pride coursed through her. At the same time she was aware of a numbing detachment. This detachment helped her get through a lot of life's main events. Train your mind on the importance of this day, this moment, she thought. Don't lose the experience.

She realized that Steve's hair was streaked with silver and his face was deeply creased. Why hadn't she noticed that before? She lowered her eyes at the intensity of his blue gaze when it locked for a few seconds onto hers, before he turned his attention to his wife, now sitting beside him on the worn bench across the aisle.

"To have and to hold..." the priest intoned. It was almost over. Tally was whispering her vows. Scott looked strong and loving and protective. That was good. His voice was firm, unwavering.

"I now pronounce you," and they were husband and wife, making a happy exit into the bright sunshine. France felt the deep bass of the organ reverberating in her chest, as the strains of the music rattled the windows.

Scott's best man came up and offered her his arm and she gratefully accepted it. They stepped down the aisle, and France shielded her eyes against the blinding August sun with her hand.

"How are you all?" she greeted a cluster of friends, squaring her shoulders slightly.

"Tally is so beautiful," gushed her old friend Maggie. "She is you made over."

"Thank you, darlin'. She does favor me a tad," France agreed, smiling, turning her head to find

Tally in the crowd. "Please excuse me for just a minute."

She was steeling herself for the receiving line and the reception. It was at times like this that she blessed her mama a million times over for her endless reminders of proper behavior and decorum. It stood her in good stead before; it was her bedrock on a day like today. Not one soul present would ever guess that she and Steve did not share the most amicable relationship in the world, or that Steve's wife was ever anything but a cherished friend.

"Thank you, Mama." France whispered the words as a quiet little prayer before she turned to greet more guests.

It was only here, on the beach, with the brilliant sun melting into the horizon that she could relax and let down her guard. She sensed her pent-up emotions releasing their grip, washing and rolling off of her like the waves foaming over the hard-packed sand in front of her, taking her feelings, thoughts and emotions and the Pandora's box that held her memories.

It all began here, she thought. Right here, on this beach, twenty-two years ago.

CHAPTER TWO

1968

The July sun was cooking the sand as Steve Marshall tried to catch up to his friend, Charlie, who was running up the beach ahead of him. Steaming heat waves blurred the beachgoers in the distance as Steve threw his towel down and jumped on it to cool his bare feet before proceeding.

"Charlie! Hold up!" His voice was almost suspended in the thick, still air. He could see Charlie pause a few yards away, standing on his own towel. He sprinted to catch up to him. They both broke into a run toward their waiting group of friends and the cooler sand by the surf.

Both men were possessed of the easy confidence of youth. Tall and muscular, their bodies were hardened from sports and surfing. Steve was the taller and better looking of the two, with black hair, piercing blue eyes and an engaging smile. Charlie was not as strikingly good-looking, but his warm brown eyes, sandy hair and laconic wit endeared him to all who knew him. They were wearing brightly colored "jams", long, loose bathing trunks that were the mark of locals.

Steve noticed a slender, pale guy in a tight-fitting "Speedo" trying to talk to a group of girls as they walked by and he nudged Charlie.

"Poor guy," Charlie laughed. Being cool was one of the primary goals on a hot summer day in 1968. "Speedo" bathing suits on the beach were not cool.

This Saturday morning their crowd was bigger than usual, tending to swell on the weekends. Almost everyone in their group was a college student, most attending the Norfolk branch of the College of William and Mary. Life in the summer in this small southeastern resort town was as carefree as it would ever be for any of them. The war in Vietnam was a dark cloud on the horizon; several of their friends were serving over there, and one girl lost her boyfriend in the conflict. The beach had a way of taking the immediacy out of everything, so that every person sitting on their bright beach towels listening to radio music blaring hit songs was living life fully and in the moment.

"Walker said that he's going to get a bonfire going tonight... are you going to come?" It was Marilyn, a pretty blonde Steve occasionally dated. Steve glanced at Charlie, who shook his head.

"I'm not sure," Steve answered.

"Can you rub this on my back?" She tossed a bottle of iodine-tinged baby oil at him, and patted the towel next to her.

Steve knelt down and squirted the oil on her shoulders, working it into her skin, warm from the sun beating down upon them. He decided to ignore the look on Charlie's face. Charlie teased Steve mercilessly about Marilyn. She was sweet and funny, but there was no chemistry, at least not for him.

He continued to massage the oil down her shoulder blades, wishing that he could feel more excited about her.

He paused when he spotted a cluster of people down the beach slightly north of where they were.

"Don't stop," Marilyn murmured. "That feels so good."

He wasn't paying attention.

"Charlie..." he said. Marilyn glanced over her shoulder and her eyes followed his gaze.

Charlie was standing at the epicenter of a circle of girls browning their backs on their towels in the sand, a human dart in the middle of a bull's eye. He sighed heavily, picking his way through the littered towels and dropped on his knees next to Steve.

"This better be important. I was working some of the old Watkins magic on Carol over there," he raised his bottle of Coke her way, as though making a toast, " and she is about to be mine."

"Yeah, right," Steve muttered. "Do you remember that cute girl with the dark hair we see every year?"

"She's a kid, moron. There are laws against that."

"She's not a kid anymore. Look at her. She's beautiful."

"She's a kid. You could have any of the babes on this beach. Marilyn here is salivating to have you." Marilyn tried to pretend she didn't hear, but her cheeks flushed with embarrassment. "So stick with someone your own age. Cradles are not meant to be robbed."

"Be back," Steve said as he got up. He heard Charlie snort in disgust as he left.

He walked down to the water before he headed up the beach. The water was so warm it felt like bath water. Little bubbles formed in the wet sand where sand fleas made their tunnels as the tide receded. Tidal pools created rivulets leading back into the water and patches of smooth sand were mixed in with patches of small rock and broken shells.

He felt good breaking away from the group. He wasn't in the mood for mindless chatter, but he wasn't sure what he really felt he was in the mood for. He and Charlie worked most of the summer at a local surf shop. He had just graduated with honors with a degree in business, but was heading to Rhode Island at the end of the summer for Officer Candidate School and a career in the Navy. He recently found out that he was color blind, which dashed his boyhood dream of being a pilot. The disappointment weighed heavily on him. He was able to sign on into another program, but it marred his excitement.

As he walked he thought about Charlie. They had grown up together, best friends since elementary school. Now Charlie was heading to Chicago for a few months of training for a large corporation. He wasn't even sure where they would send him next. Life would be weird without Charlie, Steve thought. He was looking forward to the Navy, but kind of hated the changes that were happening at lightning speed in his life.

He glanced back toward the kids down the beach. Some were finishing school, but many were graduated and heading toward the next chapter of their lives. He realized that this would be the last summer that his life would be this way, this day in, day out of work and play in the golden sand on this golden beach. Frowning, he turned north and headed with purpose toward the small, dark-haired girl standing at the shore.

France was cooling her feet in the shallows, allowing the surf to foam around her ankles. She felt uncharacteristically out of sorts. The trip from

Richmond had taken an inordinate amount of time, and the car was hot and uncomfortable. She'd endured her loathsome nine-year-old brother and his friend about as much as she could, with their stupid punching and shoving the whole trip down. As soon as they pulled into the sandy driveway of the cottage, she jumped out of the car, hauling her battered old suitcase to her room. She hurriedly unpacked, peeling off the blouse and shorts from her sticky skin and pulling on her bathing suit.

"Mama, do you need me to help?" She could hear her mother downstairs, pulling sheets off of the furnishings and turning on ancient floor fans.

Her mother eyed her thoughtfully. "I don't guess so. Go on down to the beach."

Thank you, thank you, thank you, France thought fervently. She grabbed a towel and a small ice chest filled with small bottles of Coke and slipped out the door.

The sand was hot, burning the soles of her feet, but a slight cooling breeze greeted her as she got near the water. She stood at the edge, filling her lungs with salt air. It always felt so good to get to the sea. The air at the farm was muggy but at least fresh. But the city air was dirty and oily and the exhaust from the heavy traffic heading south was oppressive.

"Move!" Her brother Will and his friend pushed past her, lugging their canvas rafts to the water. She scowled at them and turned her attention back to the ocean. They were yelling and laughing, jumping noisily onto their rafts and riding the waves into the shore.

She saw a tall, handsome boy in red jams making his way toward her. She recognized him from years past. She remembered seeing him when she was really little, with his family on the beach. He always had his fat friend with him, and then, one summer, the boys were tall and the friend was no longer pudgy, and they came without their parents. She'd thought they were good-looking and worldly, and watched them from a distance, always surrounded by pretty girls. Now the best looking one was heading straight toward her.

"Will! Watch out!" Her eyes widened in horror as Will and his raft were upended by a wave, slamming into the boy. She saw him almost topple, but quickly recover. She ran up to him.

"You apologize. Now." She glared at Will, who glared back before charging into the surf.

"I am so sorry. My brother is such a brat."

"I'm okay…no harm done." The smile that lit up Steve's face was genuine, catching her off guard.

"Are you sure?" She couldn't think of anything else to say.

"I'm fine. Really. It would take more than a kid to take me down."

She looked at him uncertainly. Was he joking?

"I'm really sorry." She looked at his leg. An angry red scratch trailed up toward his knee. "You're hurt. I've got ice in the cooler."

"I'm not hurt… but you can give me some ice, if you insist."

"I do. I insist."

They sat down on her towel, and she looked shyly at him sideways, busying herself by wrapping ice in Will's tee shirt.

"Here," she offered. He took the bundle of ice and applied it to his wound.

"What's your name?" he asked.

"Lucy Frances Ridley, but everyone calls me France."

"I'm Steve. Steve Marshall. Nice to meet you."

She smiled. "Nice to meet you too. I've seen you here before."

"I grew up not far from here. I come all the time."

"Don't you have a friend? Is he here?"

"Yeah, Charlie. He's down the beach with some of our friends."

"Oh."

"Where did you grow up?"

"Richmond. Actually, just outside Richmond, on a farm. Outside Richmond." That didn't come out right.

"Okay," he said thoughtfully. "So, what are you doing here?"

"We have a summer place, right up there," she waved in the general direction of the cottage. "We come every year for a few weeks."

"Yeah, I remember seeing you."

"You do?" She was surprised.

"Well, yeah," Steve tried to recover. "You remember the families that come every year."

"Oh."

They fell silent.

"So, what are you going to do in the fall?" He found himself praying that she was at least eighteen. He was trying to mentally calculate her age in terms of how many years he remembered seeing her on the beach.

"I graduated from high school last June and I'm supposed to go to secretarial school in the fall in Richmond. I've got a job in my daddy's law office when I'm done."

He felt an odd twinge of disappointment that she wasn't going to college, coupled with relief that she wasn't still in high school. Her accent was a good Richmond accent, well bred.

"What about you?" she was asking.

Steve bit his lip. "I just finished the college of William and Mary. I'm heading up to Newport,

Rhode Island for some schooling with the Navy. I'm joining their Intel program."

France circled her arms around her knees, drawing them up to her chin. Steve got to his feet, extending his hand to pull her up.

"Do you feel like meeting some of my friends?" Steve asked. "You already know who Charlie is."

She nodded. "Okay." She waved toward Will, pointing down the beach. "Be back in a minute. I'm going for a walk."

Will made a face at her, and he and his friend laughed.

She rolled her eyes.

They walked down the beach together. The tide was coming in and the waves were gaining strength. The grey shadow of a Navy destroyer glided seamlessly along the horizon. In their path a carefully sculpted sand castle was reduced to a swirling mass by a large wave. Steve grabbed her small hand in his and they stepped around it.

CHAPTER THREE

"You're not going out with that boy again, are you?" Although Mrs. Ridley had thrown it out as a question, France knew she meant it more as a directive.

"As a matter of fact, I am," she answered, adding, "ma'am," in hopes that a small attempt at deferential politeness would stave off a confrontation.

"Carter...." Mrs. Ridley looked imploringly at her husband, who put down his newspaper and looked squarely at his daughter.

"Honey, you have seen that boy every day for over two weeks now, and your mama and I..." he looked over at his wife, who nodded once in agreement, "feel that he's a trifle old for you."

"But Daddy!" France was kneeling beside him now, her hand on his arm. "You don't understand. He is leaving in two more weeks and *I will never see him again.* What do you expect me to do? Stay in with you and mama every night? I'm eighteen. There's nothing wrong with having fun, is there? Besides, we're just going to a party. It's at someone's house. I won't be late."

"Where is this party?" France could always work her father over; with her mother it was a different story.

"It's in Norfolk. It's a farewell party. It's a week night, and everyone is starting to leave for their jobs or grad school." She looked alarmed. "You're not going to tell me I can't go, are you?"

"When is this Steve leaving for Rhode Island?"

"He's leaving in two weeks."

Her parents looked at each other.

"I guess you can go. Just be in at a decent hour. We know you came in past midnight night before last."

"I will, Daddy, I promise. Thank you." She hugged her father, ignoring her mother's narrowed eyes.

"I know, I know," Carter Ridley said as France dashed upstairs.

"I'll be glad when the summer is over and she's back in Richmond," Anne Ridley said resignedly.

France was looking at the clothes in her closet, wishing she had thought to bring a few more dresses with her. So far, she'd just been going to parties on the beach, so it didn't matter. But tonight she wanted to really look good.

She reached in and pulled out a red cotton mini-dress in a Hawaiian print. It would have to do. Red was a good color for her, giving her confidence. Her confidence needed a little boosting with this group. She was well aware that she was the youngest and least educated among them. Back home she was the center of attention in all her social activities. She was starting to find out what it was like to feel out of her league.

She slipped the dress over her head and scrutinized herself in the mirror. Her skin glowed bronze in the fading daylight and her short, dark hair, still damp from the shower, was shiny. She dabbed a small amount of powdered blush on her cheeks with a little puff, and swiped some pale pink lipstick on to her lips and pressed them together.

She heard a short knock at the door and waited for her mother to call her, adding a few well-timed extra seconds before she started downstairs. Not one of her suitors ever had the impression that she was waiting for him by the door.

"Hi," she said sweetly as she came down the stairs. The overhead lamplight created a halo over Steve's head. Daddy was beside him, newspaper in hand. She felt Mama's eyes sweeping over her outfit. France avoided the "too short" message emanating from her mother by giving her a quick hug, pecking her father on the cheek, and tugging Steve out the door by the arm.

"France, remember what we said!" her father called after her.

"I know. We'll be home early," she said breezily.

"What was that all about?" Steve asked when they were pulling out of the driveway.

"Oh, nothing. They just don't want me to come in real late." She made a point of looking out the window.

They drove on in silence, heading toward the golf courses and hotels of the resort before maneuvering onto the interstate.

"So," began Steve. "You've never told me about your farm in Richmond." He smiled. "You don't look like a farm girl."

France smiled back. "Well, I am. Not much to tell, really. It's just a big old farmhouse, about fifteen miles outside the city. It's been in Daddy's family forever."

"Do you have animals?"

"We used to have some horses, but not anymore. He grows tobacco and rotates the fields, but that's about it."

"Sounds like a nice place to grow up."

"Well, it was."

The scenery was thinning into neighborhoods and farmsteads.

"Did you have to do chores?"

France nodded. "Of course…we worked hard, all of us. There were lots of stalls to muck out."

"Well…I have to tell you, I'm impressed. The most I ever had to do was mow the lawn…if I couldn't get Grady to do it."

"Who's Grady?"

"My kid brother…you might get to meet him before I leave."

France frowned.

"Come here," Steve said softly. She slid over next to him, and he stroked her hair, one hand on the steering wheel. "What are you thinking about?"

"I was thinking about…"

"What?"

She winced. "I don't know…just wondering if I'll ever see you again, after the summer is over." She turned to look at him, trying to read him.

"I'll be back for a few weeks next summer."

She stiffened slightly.

"Come on, France. Let's not get into any discussions right now."

"That's fine," she answered, keeping her voice as even as possible. "I'm looking forward to school in the fall. I really can't wait to get back to Richmond."

Steve's brows drew together, and for a moment, he wasn't sure what to say.

"Look, there's the Norfolk skyline."

France feigned interest. "Wow… it's kind of open, isn't it? Richmond feels like a bigger city somehow. Steve," she added. "How many people will be there tonight?"

"You're going to meet everybody tonight. I couldn't even begin to tell you how many will make it to this thing. It will be packed."

"Really?"

"Yeah. This will be the last hurrah for most of us. Charlie's leaving right after me, and a lot of the guys are leaving this weekend."

France shifted slightly in her seat. They were pulling into an older neighborhood that wrapped around a long stretch of water spanned by an iron footbridge. Gracious older houses lined the street that ran parallel to the grassy banks. Steve eased the car into a small available spot. Cars were parked along the streets for blocks. They could hear music coming from the side yard of an imposing Victorian house.

Steve came around and opened the door for France. She looked at him appraisingly. He was wearing a crisp, blue Oxford cloth shirt with a button-down collar, khaki Bermudas and leather Sperries, without socks. He was tall and tan with the clearest blue eyes she had ever seen. He smelled like salt air and bay rum and she suddenly felt very shy. He grabbed her hand and pulled her toward the noise of the party.

As they entered, they edged past clusters of people grouped on a flagstone patio and wormed their way toward a sea of familiar faces from their beach group.

"Cradle robber!" shouted a booming voice from behind them. Charlie grabbed Steve in a headlock. "How ya doin', France?"

"Hey, Charlie!" she smiled her brightest smile. She could feel that she was being sized up by a number of people. "I'm doing *great*."

Steve looked at her with interest, watching a group of girls nearby. He realized, with surprise, that they were jealous. Tiny little France with her coppery skin, sparkling dark eyes and dazzling smile had center stage. There wasn't a girl there who could compete with her. He moved in close to her, suddenly feeling territorial.

"Let's get something to drink, okay?" He navigated her through the crowd toward a table set up with bottles.

Someone put *Sealed with a Kiss* on the stereo and several couples moved toward a clearing on the patio and started to dance. Steve pulled her along with him and held her as they moved slowly in rhythm to the music. Her arms were draped around his neck and his hands were around her waist. She pressed her head against his chest, closing her eyes. She could feel his heart beating against her temple.

Steve pulled her closer and she felt her pulse quicken. The lights of the night were floating around them and the music was turned up to full volume.

I don't wanna say goodbye for the summer..."

The words of the song wafted above the melody into the trees over their heads. France burrowed closer into Steve's chest. In front of them a few boys were having an argument. Behind them they could hear a girl throwing up noisily in the bushes. But when Steve pressed his lips onto the top of her head, she was only aware of the two of them, dancing away on a summer night.

CHAPTER FOUR

"Doesn't the sun ever shine around here?" France slammed the kitchen door behind her, glaring at the rain streaming down the windowpanes.

Mrs. Ridley looked up at her from the pile of clothes she was folding. She opened her mouth to say something, but decided against it. Her daughter didn't need to be reminded that the weather had been perfect until this morning. Tonight was the last night before Richmond, and the last night Steve would be in Virginia Beach. Everyone was packing it up tomorrow.

France stepped out onto the beach, greeted by wind gusts and leaden skies and rain pelting her skin. Last night she and Steve were lying on a large blanket, looking at the stars twinkling over the night sky. They started kissing, when Steve jumped to his feet, brushing sand from his clothes.

"We've got to go."

"Why?" She remained on the blanket. She pushed up, propping her head on one hand. "What's the hurry? I've got at least another hour."

"Well, I don't. I've got some things I need to take care of… I haven't packed yet."

She still didn't move. "Why are you doing this? Don't you like me?"

Steve stood over her. He was silhouetted against the star-studded sky and she couldn't see his face.

"I *do* like you," his voice floated down to her. "A little too much. And *that's* why we've got to go."

"Well, I'm not ready to go yet." She sounded childish, resisting his attempts to pull her up.

"Suit yourself. I need to go." He was already walking up the beach.

"Don't leave me! Wait!" She jumped up and sprinted up behind him, frustrated and angry.

He laughed. "France, you live right there." The lights from her family's cottage were glimmering behind the dunes. "What do you care if I leave you?"

"I do care. I don't want you to leave me."

Steve took it at face value. "You'd be okay, either way. You're a tough girl. No one needs to tell you that."

"Not that tough," she tried to say. But he was already halfway up the beach.

When she got back the house was quiet, except for the steady whir of the washing machine. Her cheeks were flushed from being outdoors, her hair was windblown.

The clock in the kitchen was ticking loudly on the wall, ticking away the seconds of her happiness.

Richmond, she thought glumly. What was in Richmond for her?

"Oh, there you are, dear," her mother said, entering the room. She looked her over. "I wondered where you went…how was it out there?"

"Nasty," said France shortly.

"Where are you going tonight?" she said, trying to change the subject.

"I don't know," France said wearily. "He said something about the Lighthouse…"

"The Lighthouse? That's a nice restaurant. Don't you remember? We ate there two summers ago," Mrs. Ridley said cheerfully.

"I don't remember. Anyway, that's where we're going." France trudged upstairs.

Anne Ridley watched her go up, twisting her mouth reflectively. It wasn't that she didn't like Steve, she thought. He was certainly well-mannered and from a good family. He was just a little too old for France…and France was *so* young. Naïve, actually. Her mind flitted back to a summer romance of her

27

own, when she was eighteen. Her features softened at the recollection. A young army officer, Jack Peterson. Dark-haired, good-looking. In fact, Steve reminded her a little of him. She wondered whatever had happened to him. She knew exactly where her daughter got her headstrong ways. She was so stubbornly sure that Jack loved her as much as she thought she loved him. It ended badly. She hadn't thought of Jack in years, she realized with surprise. What was that old saying about never forgetting your first love?

France poked her head downstairs. "Mama, have you seen my red dress?"

"I just finished ironing it…it's right here."

"You'll be glad to know that I'll be in early tonight. Steve has to leave at five in the morning."

"All right," Mrs. Ridley acknowledged, trying not to sound relieved. "You know, France, Newport isn't so far away that he can't come see you in Richmond."

"He won't, Mama. He could even go to Viet Nam. He's not going to have time to come to see me in Richmond. It's over, after tonight." She sounded so miserable that her mother's heart went out to her.

You have no idea how this feels, France thought. How could I ever expect you to understand?

Steve checked outside the window as he emerged from the shower, vigorously drying his hair. Damn, he thought. Too bad the weather was so lousy.

His suitcases were stacked by the door, ready for tomorrow's early exit. He slapped some bay rum around his neck and finished dressing. He glanced at his watch. It was already six-thirty. God, time went by quickly.

He grabbed a windbreaker and extra blankets and hurried to his car. The car skidded slightly as he pulled onto the road, but steadied as he accelerated. Ten minutes to the oceanfront, fifteen minutes to the Ridley cottage.

France slicked another smear of lipstick over her lips while she waited for Steve. She heard his car splash up the sandy drive and the slam of his car door as he got out.

Here goes, she thought to herself.

"France, Steve is here!" Daddy's voice came up the stairs.

She steadied herself by taking a deep breath. Please, please, please, let this night be so perfect, she prayed. She squared her shoulders and raised her chin slightly before she went downstairs.

Everyone was congregated in the small hallway. Daddy was patting Steve on the back, saying, "Best of luck in the Navy, in case we don't see you any time soon."

"Thank you, sir. It was a pleasure getting to know you…thank you for allowing me to visit."

"Steve, don't be a stranger now," Mrs. Ridley gave him a formal little hug.

 You might as well be saying 'good-bye and good riddance', thought France, annoyed.

"Are we ready?" she asked, turning to him with false brightness.

"Don't be…" started her mother, before France interrupted, "We won't."

Steve looked at her oddly as he opened the door, and steered her toward the car through the biting sand blowing around them.

She clambered in and slid over beside him, kissing him lightly when he got in.

"That was nice." He smiled appreciatively. "Where to?"

"Somewhere fun. With lots of people."

He looked surprised. "Really?"

"Mm-hmm."

"You don't want to go somewhere quiet?"

"No, not really. Let's just go somewhere so we can get back."

I'm not sure how to play this one, thought Steve. He'd never had a girl ready to get rid of him before.

"You know…" he began, trying to choose his words carefully. "I was thinking that we could go for a walk on the beach. It could be fun."

"We'll get soaked."

"I've got coats in the back. If it gets too bad, we'll turn around."

She shrugged. "Fine by me."

He stopped the car about ten blocks down from her house.

"The rain has all but stopped, but here," he said, handing her a rain jacket. "Just in case."

The winds blasted them as they got past the dunes. Holding hands, they ran down the wind-whipped beach. There was something exhilarating and terrifying about being out there. The surf was pounding the shore, sending foam onto the packed sand, each wave crashing down with such force that they could almost feel the ground move. Low-lying clouds scudded across the sky, obliterating the stars.

France held tightly to Steve's hand. She felt vulnerable and very small out here in this wild weather. The lamplight from the beach houses behind the dunes seemed miles away, as though civilization and safety couldn't quickly be reached.

Steve held her close. "Are you doing okay?" His voice was carried away on the wind.

"I'm ready to go back," she tried to say.

"What?"

"I want to go back now," she tried to say above the wind.

"I know where we can go." He pulled her toward the dunes and safety.

He led her to a small, shingled house behind a larger house that fronted the street. The path was barely discernible, obscured by the windswept sand, dimly lit by the faint streetlight.

"What is this?"

"This is a house that Charlie and I watch for the owners when they're away," he answered, coaxing the large old-fashioned key into the lock. "Don't worry," he laughed, seeing the look on her face. "We have permission."

The swollen door resisted opening and shuddered as he shoved it to get in. He reached for the light switch and flipped it. It was a small room, with washed pine walls and scrubbed bare floors protected only by a tattered coir rug. Steve walked to the fireplace and started to lay a fire.

France sat on a small couch and pulled the quilt that was hanging over the back of it around her shoulders.

"Do you come here often?" She asked sarcastically.

"If you mean with other girls, not often," he tried to answer honestly.

A small blaze came to life in the grate.

"Bingo! I've got some beer in the car. Be right back."

France shifted closer to the fire. A faint warmth started to spill into the room.

Steve blew back into the house, holding a small cooler. He sank onto the couch next to her, reached in and pulled out two frosty bottles of beer.

"Here you go," he said, opening it up and offering one to her.

"Thanks." She traced a path with her finger onto the frosty glass.

"To a great summer," he whispered, clinking his bottle against hers.

"To a great summer," she returned, trying to smile.

He put his arm around her, drawing her next to him.

"You know I'm going to miss you." He planted a kiss on her forehead.

She took a small sip of beer, feeling the chilly bite of the beer chasing across her tongue.

"I will miss you, too."

"Look at me." He tilted her chin toward him. "I'm really glad we met. I'm not just saying it."

"I know. I am, too."

"There's always next summer. You'll be back down here, a year of school under your belt. I will be back, to see my folks."

"Something to look forward to," she said flatly.

"We knew this was coming, we knew it all along. Didn't we?"

"Yes, Steve. Yes we did." There was the slightest trace of defiance in her tone.

"Come here," and he kissed her, hard. She quickened, and he pulled her close. His hands moved over the curves of her body and he found himself struggling to pull off her clothes. He was breathing so quickly he thought his heart would pound out of his chest. Her breath was coming in short quick gasps.

"Stop," she whispered, but she didn't try to push him away. "Stop, Steve, don't," but she said it without conviction. He kissed her neck, her shoulders, her breasts, and pushed her gently down onto the couch, positioning himself on top of her. She felt as though she was being carried away on a rollercoaster, the pain was so exquisite, and she whimpered when they finished and he rolled heavily off of her. She was shaking. He turned to her, pulling her against his chest, and held her in his arms.

"That was the first time for you, wasn't it?" he whispered.

She shook her head yes. A small tear trickled down her cheek.

He didn't say anything back, but stroked her hair in light, tender strokes.

They could hear a clock chiming somewhere in the house. He looked at his watch.

"It's only eight-thirty," he said softly. "Do you want to stay a little while longer?"

She shook her head no. "I think I need to go home."

"Are you okay?" His voice rose slightly.

"I'm fine." She wasn't sure what to say to him. She wasn't even sure what she was feeling herself.

"Okay." He sounded uncertain.

Wordlessly they dressed, folded the quilt, ad banked the fire. A few embers burned red through the ash.

They slipped into the night, Steve locking the door behind them. The wind had died down, but the air was bracing, shockingly cold after being in the warmth.

The car creaked to a halt in her driveway, and he walked her up the path to the house. Standing in a pool of light, he kissed her.

"You mean a lot to me...I won't forget you," he whispered in her ear. "I'm glad I was your first."

"Please don't," she pleaded. It was all she could manage as she turned to go into the house. She didn't even look back to see his face.

They left the next morning, exactly at nine. The old house looked somewhat forlorn, like a beloved pet that wasn't ready or willing to be left behind. The sun was peeking out from behind a few fluffy clouds, promising a perfect beach day.

France sat in the front seat, next to her mother, idly watching the scenery fly by. They were heading west on Shore Drive, where the state park became a tunnel of trees before opening into a small bay front community.

The boys in the back seat were making a game of spotting license plates. France was absorbed in her own thoughts; she half expected to see Steve's car passing them on the highway.

But Steve was halfway to Rhode Island by now. With a start she opened her bag and rummaged around for a scrap of paper. Her address and phone number. She'd forgotten to give it to him.

He couldn't reach her now if he tried. She sank down into her seat and pressed her face against the half open window.

It really was good-bye.

CHAPTER FIVE

September 1968
Richmond

France eased her car onto the gravel next to her mother's station wagon, edging past the late blooming roses lining the fence around the house. It was Friday, and she had just wrapped up the third week of school. With classes beginning every morning at 8:30 a.m. and finishing up at 4:30 p.m., she was left to battle the worst of the city traffic before reaching her Henrico County farm.

Her head was swimming with legal terminology, ethics and public relations, and she was relieved to see the Richmond skyline recede and the fields of tobacco and fallow corn come into view, a sight that told her she was almost home.

She could see the white farmhouse at the end of the long lane of cedar trees that led to it. It was a clapboard house on an English basement, flanked by rows of ancient boxwood. The grounds were permeated with the smell so peculiar to historic Virginia; the mingled scent of boxwood and old brick.

It was early fall and the smell of wood smoke hung in the air, a reminder of the two hundred years' worth of fires that had burned in the old brick fireplaces of 'Clifton'.

'Clifton' had two huge double doors that opened into a large entrance hall, with a wide staircase to the left. Straight ahead another set of double doors led to the kitchen garden in the back, which, according to Grandmama Ridley, allowed the prevailing breezes from the cedar lane to funnel into the house and provide an early form of air conditioning, a welcome relief from the muggy Virginia summers.

Today France felt particularly weary. The air conditioning in her car wasn't working, and the hot wind from the open windows on the drive home left her feeling grimy and fatigued.

She stooped to pat the head of her Golden Retriever before entering the house. He lifted his great head for one brief minute before dropping it back down on the brick walkway.

"You're really late today," her mother said from the kitchen when she heard her come in.

"It was awful today," France answered. "The traffic was backed up for miles."

"Daddy called a few minutes ago...he's running behind, too. Are you feeling all right?" Mrs. Ridley looked at France in consternation.

"Not really. I'm exhausted. I think I'll lie down for a few minutes before dinner."

"All right, honey. I'll call you when it's ready."

France trudged up the stairs to her room, kicking off her shoes when she entered. She flopped onto her bed, sinking into the featherbed on top of the mattress. The pillows were so cool and sweet against her hot cheek and her eyes felt so heavy she could barely keep them open. Swirls of dust danced in the rosy shaft of sunlight that came through the open window as she fell into a deep sleep. She slept so soundly she didn't hear her mother enter the room to call her for dinner.

When she did awake, it was well past nine o'clock. She slipped out of bed and stood at the door. Her parents were talking low in the parlor, and she thought she heard them say her name. As she flipped on the bathroom light, she caught a glimpse of her image in the mirror.

Oh, my Lord, she thought. She could almost hear her grandmother's gravelly voice: "You look like Death warmed over". I do, she thought. I do look like Death warmed over. Her face looked pinched and drawn, sallow under her fading tan and her eyes were smudged. She turned the chrome handles of the bathtub on, peeled off her clothes and got in, allowing the warm spray of water to wash over her body and stream through her hair.

She toweled off and considered going downstairs to scrounge for food, but the thought of eating wasn't appealing for some reason, even though she was almost dizzy with hunger. Without bothering to take off her robe she crawled back into bed and sank into a dreamless sleep.

She awoke the next morning to brilliant sunshine streaming through her window. She felt empty and ravenous for having not eaten the night before, but the second she got out of bed she was racked with waves of the worst nausea she had ever known. She ran for the bathroom and slumped over the commode and vomited. The porcelain tile was so cool against her bare knees, and she was shaking all over

What in God's name is going on with me? Her mouth felt dry and the leftover vomit in her mouth burned her tongue. She laid her head on the edge of the toilet praying for the nausea to subside. She couldn't imagine anything feeling worse than this.

The day for Steve started out like any other day, with classes and meetings and training schedules. He enjoyed the challenges presented to him and thrived on the daily routine. He was excited to go in every day. When he wasn't studying he would meet some of his new buddies for a beer at the Officer's Club. He was starting to date a cute girl named Cindy, a pediatric nurse at the base clinic.

It was lunch before he had time to swing by and pick up his mail. There were two letters from Charlie. He read the letters with amusement, and almost laughed out loud when he read about Charlie's latest weekend adventure. Trouble seemed to find Charlie wherever he went. It looked like Charlie would be heading off to California after his training in Chicago. Lucky guy.

He was heading for the mess hall when a young enlisted man tapped him on the shoulder.

"Sir, you got a phone call about an hour ago. Here's the number."

Steve looked at the writing on the piece of paper and didn't recognize it. His first reaction was that his father was ill, but it wasn't a Tidewater, Virginia number.

"Did they say if it was an emergency?" he asked.

"No, sir. They just asked that you call when you get a chance."

"Did they leave a name?"

"No sir, they didn't."

Steve shrugged. "Okay…thanks."

He folded the paper and stuck it in his pocket and went on to join his friends in the mess hall.

When he got back to his room later that night he remembered the phone call. He pulled the paper from his pocket and looked at the numbers. 703. A middle Virginia area code.

He put the paper on the nightstand and carefully dialed the number. He listened to the ring of the call whirring in his receiver, tracing the BELL SYSTEM PROPERTY-NOT FOR SALE letters imprinted in the black housing of the phone with his finger, waiting for someone to answer.

"Hello?"

"Hello, this is Steve Marshall...someone called me from this number?"

There was a brief pause, a woman's voice, stiffly polite. "Hello, Steve. This is Mrs. Ridley. Let me call France. One moment, please."

France? Why would she be trying to call him?

He could hear Mrs. Ridley muffle the receiver. "France! Can you come to the phone? We've got Steve is on the line."

After a few minutes, he heard France pick it up.

"Mama, I've got it," then a click.

"France? Hey, how are you? What's going on? Why did you call me?" He heard France's mother fumbling on the extension, and a click when she finally hung up.

"We need to talk."

"What do we need to talk about?" His voice sounded faint.

"Steve, I'm not going to mess around, so I am just going to come out with it." She drew a deep breath. "Steve, I'm pregnant."

CHAPTER SIX

France was in her upstairs bathroom splashing cool water on her face when she heard a firm knock at the front door. She'd been pacing around nervously for the better part of the afternoon watching the dirt road for the clouds of dust that signaled a car was arriving. When she wasn't pacing, she was checking herself in the mirror.

She heard her mother's light tread going down the center hall to answer it.

"Steve! Welcome to 'Clifton!'" the warm welcome resounded in the hallway.

France was dreading this moment. She was convinced that she would know everything that was going through Steve's mind the second she saw him. With trepidation, she crept down the stairs. She saw the top of his dark head towering over Mama's.

He looked up. "Hi, France."

Her mother reached out with one hand, waving France closer.

"Hi." She searched his face. He looks scared, she thought, almost as scared as me.

Steve was surprised at how worn she looked. She was smiling, but her eyes weren't.

His eyes traveled up the sweep of the hallway, alighting for one brief second in the direction of her waist.

"Steve, do come in and have some iced tea. I know you must be tired." Mama was utilizing her best take-charge voice; Steve had no choice but to follow. If the Russians themselves ever found their way up the driveway to invade 'Clifton', France was convinced her mother would be offering them iced tea.

"We'll take it on the porch," Mama continued, prodding France forward with her eyes.

"This way," France said simply, leading him through the house to the wide covered porch that led to a brick patio. Dark green rocking chairs with blistered paint and curling strands of wicker were lined up like so many residents of an old folk's home. France ushered him to one and motioned for him to sit down.

The woods that ran along the edge of the field were burnished in autumn colors. It was one of those warm, humid Virginia fall days with the vague promise of chilly weather hidden in the balmy breeze.

"Did you have a nice drive?" she asked awkwardly.

"Not too bad," he answered. "It's always congested around D.C."

They lapsed back into silence.

"Here we are," said her mother, pushing the screen door open with her elbow, carrying a tea tray with four glasses and a frosty pitcher of amber-colored tea.

"There are only three of us, Mama. You expecting somebody?"

"Your daddy, darlin'," she smiled warmly. "He's coming home early, to talk to Steve."

Steve blanched. "Won't you have some lemon?"

Steve only had four days off, so the wedding was planned for Sunday afternoon at the beach chapel. All Saturday afternoon Ridley and Talbot relatives passed through 'Clifton' to meet France's intended.

"I'm warning you," she said to him quietly when there was a lull between visitors, "you are going through trial by fire." She was only half-joking.

"Great," he whispered back. "Am I passing?"

"I'm not sure yet," she smiled, trying to sound playful. "I'll give you your grade when it's over."

Steve's laugh sounded forced to both of them.

He left in the early evening, to stay with his parents. Charlie was flying in to stand in as his best man.

She walked him to the door.

"I'll see you tomorrow," he said as he leaned in to kiss the top of her head.

She nodded. "Have a safe trip."

"I will."

She pushed the door closed softly behind him.

The last guest left at eleven. France was trying to pack the last items for her trip when Mama knocked lightly at the door.

"Need any help?"

"I think I've got it," France answered, her voice heavy with weariness.

Mrs. Ridley sat on the bed. "Steve is a good man," she said simply.

"How does Daddy feel about him?"

Her mother's thoughts touched lightly on the anguished rantings she's been subjected to these past few weeks.

"He feels as I do…he's a fine young man from a good family with a promising future. He fit in nicely with everyone today, didn't you think?"

"What if he doesn't love me, Mama? And what if I don't love him?"

Her mother wanted to say something about the wisdom of having thought about that last summer, but checked herself. "Love grows, my darling. You and Steve haven't had time to cultivate love, but it can, and will, grow over time. It's a lot of hard work, especially under…these circumstances. But you both need to commit yourselves to make sure that it will grow."

"And what if it doesn't?"

"Well, I would expect that would depend on the maturity of the people involved. Steve is certainly doing the honorable thing…"

"I'm not ready, mama. I never meant for this to happen…"

"Lucy Frances," her mother said seriously. "This isn't just about you and Steve anymore. You are having a baby, and that means there is more to this than just you and Steve. It means that you might have to think about someone other than yourself. And it really means that you will need to grow up mighty fast."

"What if… I didn't have the baby? There was a girl…at school…"

Her mother grabbed her by the shoulders, digging her fingers into them. "That is not even a remote possibility. It goes against everything we believe in and don't you ever forget it. I hope to God that that was just your fear talking…"

"I'm sorry. I don't know how I feel. I think I love Steve. But I'm not fooling myself that he loves me. You saw the way he acted. He doesn't want to get married. I feel like he thinks I'm trapping him into this."

France looked up at her mother.

"He's old enough to take responsibility for his actions. Now," she stood back up. "We've got a big day tomorrow. We could talk about this 'til kingdom come, but it is not going to change a thing. No one wants to get married under duress, but we all need to do what's right. I do think Steve loves you, in his way. I think he's just scared to death."

"I hope you're right," France conceded. "I mean, the part about loving me. Not the part about Steve being scared."

"I am right, precious. Get some rest."

"Goodnight, Mama. I'll go to bed in a little. I still have some things to pack."

"Don't stay up too late," her mother warned. "Oh, and France… it will all work out. You'll see. These things always do."

"I hope so, Mama. I hope so."

Moonlight streamed into the darkened bedroom at 'Clifton'. The fields beyond were gleaming blue, the tree line black against the night sky. Her bridal gown hung shimmering in the frosty light on a hanger on the door, gleaming pearly gray in the strange blue light.

France lay awake, although her eyes were heavy. She was savoring every familiar creak and shadow of the old house, and could hardly believe that she was leaving it forever. She didn't know a thing about husbands and babies. On the mantel were remnants of another life; her cheerleading megaphone, ticket stubs and wilted corsages from dances that took place only a few months ago, but felt like a hundred years ago.

Tomorrow she was getting married. She was marrying a man who didn't love her and most definitely did not want to marry her.

I am only eighteen, she thought. Only eighteen.

CHAPTER SEVEN

An off shore breeze stirred the lace curtains of the beach cottage. It was two o'clock in the afternoon and France was sitting at her wobbly dressing table, trying to put the finishing touches to her makeup. The earlier balmy warmth beckoned France to walk on the beach as soon as they arrived, flushing her cheeks and turning her skin golden.

"To veil or not to veil." Martha toyed with a piece of gauzy tulle netting, waving it like a small airplane around her sister's head.

"Not to veil." France was emphatic. "I hate hats…they just don't look right on me."

"This is not a hat, it's a *veil*. Put on your dress and we'll make the decision then."

France obediently lifted her arms and Martha slid the gown over her head and worked it down France's body.

"Oh, my Lord, honey," she said in a low voice. "You were really cutting it close. One more week and we couldn't have gotten this thing on."

They both looked at the fragile silk stretched over France's expanding waist.

Tears sprang into France's eyes. "I look horrible…I can't wear this," she waved her hand over the dress. She put her hand to her mouth. "I think I'm going to be sick."

"No, you are not, and yes, you will wear it. " Martha's voice was so firm that all France could do was stare at her and nod dumbly. "You are going to be the most beautiful bride on God's green earth, you'll see." She took her younger sister's face in her hands. "Trust me on that one. Beautiful. You hear?"

Martha pulled her over to the full-length mirror. "And you're right about the hat. I mean, the veil. It's a bit much." She held it up to France's glossy, short hair and tossed it onto the bed. "Here," she said, plucking a single red rose from a box on the dresser. "Try this," and she tucked the rose behind France's ear, deftly pinning it into her hair. "Perfect."

Steve looked haggard. The bachelor party carried over from the bars to the beach at sunrise. The beach was chilly at night, and even the warmth of the bonfire and a well-worn sweatshirt couldn't keep the cold from creeping into Steve's joints and muscles. His throat was scratchy and his eyes burned.

Could it get any damn more perfect? he thought angrily. I feel like crap.

Charlie was snoring noisily on an old rubber raft on the floor beside his bed. He'd tried hard to hold Steve up last night, to his credit. Old Charlie. What a friend. He sank back into the pillows that felt clammy and sweaty against his cheek, rough with this morning's stubble. A nasty smell of stale smoke from the fire and cigarettes intermingled with the unmistakable stench of heavy alcohol consumption breathed by men who hadn't brushed their teeth the night before.

What time was it? He had the feeling that if he could just close his eyes and go back to sleep he would wake up and it would be Monday and this whole thing would be over. He could hang out on the beach, pop a few cold ones with Charlie, and maybe catch a few waves…

Overwhelming exhaustion crept over him like fog rolling across the water. He closed his eyes. He was standing on the short brick steps saying good-bye to Cindy. He could see her big green eyes looking into his, and the subtle wash of freckles sprinkled across her creamy skin.

He wanted to break the news gently. He was going to take her for a walk, but the walk turned into dinner, dinner turned into a movie, the movie into a longer walk that ended with a lingering kiss on the steps where they stood. She was pulling him across the threshold and he was resisting. He saw the questioning look on her face.

"What's the matter? Why aren't you coming?" Her expression was sweetly quizzical. "Steve…"

"We need to talk." He cringed at the hollow sound of his voice when the words tumbled out, so weak. In all the years that followed, he would never forget the stricken look on her face.

"You're doing *what*?" The color drained from her cheeks, her eyes were round. She was trying so hard to make sense of it.

"I can explain," he fumbled, thinking, how can I explain? So incredibly weak.

"No you cannot explain. No, you cannot." Now her voice was rising, angry. She pushed him away. "*You made love to me…we…*" she fiercely brushed away tears.

He tried to take her in his arms, to hold her tightly to him.

"Get away from me. Get away. You make me *sick*." She wheeled around, slipped behind the door and slammed it shut so forcefully that the windows shook. He could hear her sobbing inside as he stood uncertainly at the door.

He had no idea how long he stood there. But when he finally turned to leave, he felt empty and deflated inside. Cindy. He wanted so badly to see her eyes sparkle at the sight of him, to feel her embrace.

He was aware of Charlie's huge hands shoving him.

"Get up!" Charlie's voice was thick. "Get up, you piece of crap! Today is your big day!"

The kitchen smelled of hot biscuits, coffee and bacon. Mrs. Marshall was standing at the stove when they stumbled in.

"Eggs and bacon are on the sideboard," she smiled as they entered.

"I can't eat, Mom," Steve said, slugging down a glass of orange juice. He grimaced as a wave of queasiness welled up within him.

"Oh, Steve," his mother looked worried. "What time did you boys get in?"

"It's okay, Mrs. Marshall," Charlie said, loading his plate up with golden, flaky biscuits. "I'm eating for two now…" He shot Steve an innocent look. "I mean, for me and Steve."

"Can I come in?" Mrs. Marshall was rapping lightly on the bedroom door.

"We've almost got him ready, Mrs. M." Charlie was straddled backwards on Steve's old desk chair, resting his head on the back of it. His hair was uncombed, his shirt unbuttoned, his tie hung loose around his neck.

Steve adjusted the last bright brass button on his white uniform. Charlie grinned approvingly.

"Oh, Steve." Mrs. Marshall clapped her hands as she entered, one little clap. "You look so *handsome.* You really do."

"He sure does clean up well," Charlie offered.

Steve's mother turned to Charlie. "Honey, would you mind?" She looked pointedly at the door. Charlie stared at her dully.

Steve started combing his hair. "I think she's telling you to get out, old buddy."

"Oh." Charlie looked startled. "Nobody has to ask old Charlie twice."

"Thank you, Charlie." Mrs. Marshall closed the door firmly behind him.

Here it comes, thought Steve. He knew the look in her eyes and the firm set of her jaw all too well.

She took a deep breath. "Steve, you have been raised to be an honorable and decent man, with high standards."

"Why do you think I'm here?"

"I can read you like a book and I don't like what I'm seeing. France deserves better." Her blue eyes, so like his own, fixed on his, forcing his attention.

He finally looked down. "What do you expect, Mom?"

"I expect you to step up to the plate and develop a better attitude. France didn't get into this by herself. I expect you to treat her well. Steve?"

"Yes ma'am."

"Don't *ma'am* me! She is a beautiful girl and will make a wonderful wife. You had *better* do right by her. You need to give love a fighting chance. Do you hear me?"""

Steve nodded. She hugged him, clasping his arm firmly on the way out.

"Do right by her," she added once more. "And I mean it. Don't think I don't."

It was three forty-five when the car bearing France and her family pulled into the oyster shell parking lot next to the church. The sky was clear and cerulean blue, an unusually warm and humid day for early November. As France stepped carefully from the car, a warm gust lifted the flower positioned so carefully in her hair. She patted it down, listening to the strains of the organ groaning from the chapel.

A few latecomers were still waiting to enter the church. She could see the groomsmen working their way toward the last of them, pointedly asking "bride or groom?" as they proffered an arm.

Oh, Daddy, she thought as she saw her father coming toward her. He smiled reassuringly, but his eyes were sad.

Feeling a slight tug on her arm, she turned to face a skinny, sunburned, freckle-faced boy of about fourteen. His suit hung loosely on his thin frame.

"I'm Grady," he said softly. His nose was peeling, a sign of many hours surfing at the Steel Pier. She guessed he was probably wishing he could be there now.

"Grady, I'm France." She extended her hand. "I was wondering when I was going to meet Steve's younger brother."

"My brother's here, in case you were worried."

"Worried? Me? Not a chance," she laughed, feeling a glimmer of her old confidence return.

"You look pretty and, uh…" he stumbled. "Welcome to the family." He looked up sharply when he heard the opening notes of *Jesu, Joy of Man's Desiring* coming from the organ. "Uh-oh. I think that means I'm supposed to take your mom in."

"Well, go." France shooed him off. As she saw her mother disappear into the sanctuary, her heart started to race.

It's time, she thought, feeling panicked. She turned to her father, who tucked her arm in his, stolidly folding his large hand over hers.

"Steady now, girl," he said firmly. Her bouquet was shaking, but she inhaled deeply, thrusting her chin out slightly.

They stood at the end of the aisle, waiting. Steve was standing resolutely at the altar, his skin flushed, flanked by Charlie, looking disheveled.

General Lee's March sounded on the organ as everyone got to their feet. All heads snapped as they looked back at her.

Her father paused. "Are you ready?"

She started to go, but he held her back.

"Are you ready?" His voice was loving, but emphatic. She realized that he was giving her a way out.

"I'm ready, Daddy. Really. I am." Her voice was determined, her eyes unwavering, staring straight down the end of the aisle. She pulled her gaze away to focus on him. "I want to do this."

"Then let's go."

Every face that turned toward her on the long way up the aisle would be burned into her memory for years to come.

This can't be happening, she thought. It was a sea of faces blurring together, with an occasional face standing out in sharp clarity. Aunt Claire. Her cousin Morgan. Some of the kids from the beach, friends of Steve's. None of her friends, though. Not one. Her family was of the mind that it would be better this way.

She became dimly aware of her feet moving in time to the music, almost gliding, carried along by her father. Steve's face moved into view, and then the minister. There was Charlie, with that funny half-smile of his. She allowed herself to look at Steve, taking in his expression. He stood tall and straight and unsmiling, his blue gaze boring into her, through her. She had a brief impulse to kick off her slippers and run, right out that door. She could almost hear the collective gasp of the congregation if she did it. As quickly as the thought entered her head, it left. The organ thundered to a stop. The nasal voice of the priest intoned, *Who gives this woman away?* She was surprised to hear her father's voice so close to her, answering, *Her mother and I do.* She felt herself being propelled toward Steve, like something precious being traded. She looked back at her father in alarm. He was already heading over to where her mother was sitting. She looked up at Steve into those impenetrable blue eyes, where nothing registered. Not hope, or happiness, or humor. She cast her eyes downward, trying to ignore the rushing in her ears. She turned toward the priest, sensing Steve turning at the same time. The ceremony began.

The small tent set up on the beach behind the cottage was swarming with people. The sun was sinking into the horizon, washing the sea with fiery rose. Candles gleamed in sand-filled hurricanes, the cheerful light dancing off of silver punch bowls.

France stole a glance at the foreign glint of the thin gold band that encircled her ring finger. Steve was chatting animatedly with a group of his friends while Charlie made his way to a gaggle of girls huddled protectively around Marilyn, who was dabbing her eyes with a wadded handkerchief.

"I always cry at weddings," she justified.

"Especially the ones where you thought you were going to be the bride," Charlie inserted, surveying the narrowed eyes of the women glaring at him. He shrugged as Marilyn dropped her jaw in protest, backing out in time to snare another glass of champagne. Almost time to deliver the toast.

"Good job, Martha," France breathed happily. She was standing by the tables draped in white linen, silver platters heaped with crab claws and succulent Lynnhaven oysters surrounded by vibrant wedges of lemon. Tiny crab cakes from Mama's family recipe were stacked on an old blue platter and there were mountains of the ubiquitous Virginia ham biscuit, which no Virginia celebration or rite of passage could do without.

"Well, you're worth it, baby sister." Martha squeezed her arm.

"It is so beautiful…it's perfect. You have such an eye."

Martha was clearly pleased with her effort. "Nothing like blue and white and silver on the beach, honey," she smiled. She rearranged some sun-bleached oyster shells around a plate. "Your boy Charlie looks like he's enjoyed the champagne a little too much."

France felt alarmed. Sure enough, Charlie was weaving toward a cluster of beach friends, glass held high above his head. His sandy hair was wind-blown, giving him the aspect of a small boy about to get into trouble. His shirt was open, his tie was hanging in a big loop around his neck.

"Oh, my Lord, France," Martha hissed. "He has been in the *water*."

Their eyes traveled down to Charlie's pant legs. They were soaked, wet sand caking his legs.

"Somebody stop him," France pleaded urgently.

It was too late. He was already tapping his glass with his spoon, clearing his throat importantly.

Steve moved in behind France, placing his hand at the small of her back. "This might not be good," he whispered.

"Can you do anything?"

"Not now, I can't."

Charlie had begun. "May I have your attention, please…?" He swayed.

France hardly breathed.

"To Steve-o and his beautiful…" Charlie had trouble forming the word. " Beautiful," he said carefully, "bride, France. She may be young, but she's a keeper. Steve-o, you're my best friend. I just want you to be happy, man. To Steve and France."

"To Steve and France." The entire company raised their glasses.

"That was *it*?" Steve asked in surprise. "That wasn't too bad, was it?" He looked at France and Martha for their feedback, and broke into the first smile he had smiled all day, a look of relief commingling with pleasure.

He looked up to see everyone watching him. He clinked his glass to France's and kissed her. Everyone applauded.

A fresh breeze whipped the awning. The cake was cut and the day was drawing to a close.

"Honey, you need to go throw your flowers at those girls over there," Martha directed.

"Oh, yeah. I guess I do need to do that. I almost forgot."

Martha turned her around, away from the group of girls jockeying for center position.

France closed her eyes and tossed her bouquet. Somewhere in the crowd she heard a male voice. "Throw it to Marilyn!" It sounded like Charlie.

The bouquet sailed up and over, and Marilyn emerged, clutching it in her upraised hand in triumph. For a split-second a look passed between them, replaced by a bright smile from both girls.

CHAPTER EIGHT

Newport, Rhode Island

It was well after dark by the time they reached their apartment in Newport. France was feeling sick the whole time, and it seemed that they needed to stop every fifty miles. Steve bore it as long as he could, but by the sixth stop he was clearly exasperated.

"Can't you control it?" he asked through clenched teeth. He was sorry the second the words left his mouth. His answer was in the pallor of her miserable little face.

"I'm sorry," he said, softening. "It's just that we have to make time, that's all. I have to start work in the morning."

"I'll try to make it," France promised. She tried to eat a cracker but it was dry and flavorless. She didn't have anything to wash it down.

"I think we can get there by nine, if we don't stop anymore," Steve said, hopefully.

She felt so rocky she couldn't answer. She stared out the window, thinking of the previous night.

Martha had decided that the cottage was where they should spend their wedding night. A small fire was crackling cheerfully in the grate when they entered and rose petals were strewn all the way to the bedroom.

"Please tell me she didn't outfit the bed with red velvet sheets," Steve snorted when he saw the rose petal path.

"Don't kill the mood," France retorted. "And wait a minute. You didn't carry me over the threshold." She looked at him expectantly.

"Okay, okay. You're right. Go back outside."

They stepped back out and he scooped her up in his arms, stumbling slightly at the base of the stairs.

"That's more like it," she murmured, clinging to his neck.

He carried her to the bed and gently rolled her on top of the mattress. They undressed wordlessly.

"Let me look at you," Steve whispered. Her breasts were large and full against the smallness of her frame, and he traced the curves of her body, so different from the girlish leanness of just a few months ago.

"Is it okay?" he said softly in her ear.

She shook her head yes.

They awakened to the slamming of a shutter against a window. The weather that had been so fair had turned savagely foul.

"Get up. We need to get on the road."

"No!" France looked at the window, cloudy with sea spray. "It's only 6:00 a.m." She'd been dreaming that storms were destroying her house, her cries for help mingling with the howling wind. "Can we stay just one more day? Please? Is there the slightest chance?"

"There's not," he said shortly. He was standing with his towel around his waist, his hair still damp from his shower.

She pulled herself up from the bed and the comfortable nest of blankets, glancing at her reflection in the mirror before padding downstairs. She fought off a wave of queasiness. Her pregnancy dictated that she never went too long without eating.

"I hope you're putting coffee on," he called from upstairs. "We'll need it."

Coffee? she thought. I don't know how to make *coffee*.

She opened the cupboard where she believed Mama kept the coffee tin. She pulled it out, studying the directions on the back. The old percolator sat on the back of the stove, but she wasn't sure how many cups of water it took.

"I'll make the coffee," Steve said with a tangible air of resignation as he entered the kitchen, yanking the tin out of her hands. "Go get dressed."

By the time they pulled out of the drive, sand was pelting the car and obscuring the cottage from her vision. Houses were flipping by as they picked up speed. The road widened from scrub pine to a sandy little neighborhood before the broad expanse of the Chesapeake Bay came into view, with rough and churning waters crested with whitecaps, or "cat's paws", as she'd grown up calling them. She saw the old weathered fishermen's restaurant, the Duck-In, tucked into the dunes to her right. She suddenly craved the Smithfield bacon and scrambled farm eggs and pancakes that were served in the cavernous old dining room overlooking the water.

"Steve?"

"Yeah?"

"I need to eat. The toast wasn't enough. I'll feel better after I eat. Can we stop? Please?" She pointed to the Duck-In.

"No, France. We're already fifteen minutes behind. You'll have to wait."

"Please, Steve. I can't wait. I need to eat now."

"Not now." His voice was firm, although he noticed the greenish cast of her skin. "After we cross the bridge tunnel. Then we'll stop."

She looked desperately at the Duck-In receding in the distance.

"Okay, what do you think?"

The single, bare light bulb protruding from the overhead fixture was the only illumination in the room.

France stood in the doorway, trying to take it in.

She managed a weak smile. "I like it."

"There's a warehouse if we need more furniture," his voice trailed. "I'll get the rest of your things."

She tried to look happy, but she was too tired to pull it off. It was so dingy, she thought. A shabby sofa took up one wall, and a tired armchair faced it. A bulky television set filled up a corner and a stereo sat on top of a makeshift bookcase, comprised of cinderblocks and plywood.

She flipped on another light to try to find a bathroom. The fixtures were antiquated, the floors and half of the wall lined with small, matte, black and white octagonal tiles. She sat on the side of the tub and turned on the water. The handles resisted being turned until she twiddled the dull chrome paddles and teased out a brownish trickle of water accompanied by a high-pitched wail. She watched the water peppering the sides of the tub, then peeled off her clothes and sank into the steamy bath.

She couldn't remember feeling so good after a good soak. Wrapped in a frayed towel she peered around the corner into the bedroom. Steve was wrestling her heavy suitcase into the room.

"This thing weighs a ton."

She was too tired to respond.

"Feeling better?"

She nodded. "So much better."

He stopped and watched her pressing the dampness out of her hair. "I put the rest of your stuff over there." He pointed to a collection of boxes and suitcases in the corner.

"Thanks," she said, trying to sound grateful.

She unzipped a small bag and rooted around for her nightgown. She pulled it over her head and folded back the sheets of the double bed and climbed in. The sheets were scratchy and smelled musty, but she was too tired to care.

By the time Steve got out of the shower she was fast asleep, with the overhead light on and the contents of her suitcase spilling out onto the floor. He shrugged, turned off the lights and slipped in beside her.

So much for night number two, he thought. At least she didn't cry when she saw the place.

CHAPTER NINE

"Oh, my gosh… that looks like my homeplace." France paused in front of the little shop on Franklin Street. Small flakes of snow swirled around her. She pointed to a large painting of a white clapboard house with Charleston green shutters, framed in spotty gold leaf.

"That?" Larkin Mason came up beside her, peering into the filmy glass window of the little store. "That's really pretty. Where did you say you grew up?"

"On a farm…outside Richmond. It even has a name. Clifton."

"Oh, my goodness. Are you okay?" Larkin's eyes grew wide with concern when she saw tears trickle down France's cheek.

"I'm fine," France answered, wiping her cheek with a mittened hand. "I don't know where that came from. I suddenly felt homesick."

"Of course you do," Larkin said soothingly. "That and hormones. I remember I cried at the drop of a hat. I cried during *commercials*."

France laughed. "That's pretty bad. I haven't quite done that, yet."

Are you going home for Thanksgiving?"

France shook her head. "Steve said we can't take the time to go home. What about you all?"

"We're not that far away, really. Connecticut. So we're packing up the boys on Wednesday and heading out."

"Lucky you. By the way, Steve said he has met your husband. I asked him if he knew him when I told him about meeting you for coffee. They have a class together…"

"Yeah, Frank said he knew Steve, but not well." She looked at France thoughtfully. "At least you got to meet most of the wives at the meet-and-greet."

"Yeah, that was fun, " France nodded. "I've only been up here a month and Steve has been busy. He works late every night."

"He does?" Larkin was a little puzzled.

"So, it's been a little lonely for me," France continued. She brightened. "I can't tell you how glad I was to have you want to go out today."

"Well, I knew that we'd have fun. To tell the truth, Frank and I don't really get out much either. Our lives revolve around the twins. You won't have much time to be lonely after the baby comes, I promise you. I'm glad you were able to go out. I needed adult companionship! I was worried I was losing my vocabulary!"

France smiled. "I don't know how you did it with twins. Did you get very…big?"

"Huge. I was twice what you are now, trust me. When are you due?"

"Not until May. Larkin, do you mind if we go in? I want to see how much that painting is."

"Where did you get that?" Steve was standing at the front door, looking at the painting hanging over the sofa. The chilly air from outdoors seemed to have blown in with him.

"I bought it today, when I was out with Larkin Mason," France answered cheerfully.

"How much was it?"

"It was ten dollars. I had some of our wedding money. I used that."

"You might want to run it by me before you go blowing money on junk."

France was immediately defensive. "It was ten dollars! We needed something on the walls around here. I like it and I miss my home. It reminded me of 'Clifton'."

Steve pushed past her toward the bedroom and France followed him in.

"I made spaghetti for dinner," she said, placatingly.

"I don't have time to eat," he answered. "I'm meeting Sam and Rob at the "O" club in fifteen minutes."

"Steve! You've been out late every night this week. Not tonight, too. Please stay home. Please." Her voice was imploring.

He gave her a long look. "I'll try to be back before nine."

"Steve. Please don't go." She watched him change his shirt, grab his keys and walk out the door. She fixed a small bowl of spaghetti, flipped on the television and sank into the sofa. After dinner the flickering of the television screen lulled her to sleep. When she awoke at ten-thirty she realized that Steve wasn't home yet. She got ready for bed and slept so soundly that she didn't hear him come in at midnight.

Thanksgiving Day dawned grey and cold. France carefully spread out and surveyed the heirloom recipes Martha had compiled for her as she prepared to cook the feast. The football game was blaring from the other room, where Steve and his buddy Dave watched television.

"You know I've never done this before," she said, peering into the living room.

Steve looked up. "You'll do fine. I have faith in you. Besides, you come from a long line of great cooks."

"That's right, I do," she agreed. "But the line is about to end right here with me."

"Oh, come ON. What kind of a call was THAT?" Steve and Dave groaned, riveted to the set.

"I'm telling you, I don't know what I'm doing," France said as she exited the room.

The two men placed themselves at the carefully set table where the turkey sat dry and forlorn at the center, flanked by a bowl of grainy mashed potatoes. A plate of biscuits, leaden and charred, was arranged on the other side. A dismal sweet potato pie with a creased and runny filling and a blackened crust filled the small apartment with its burnt aroma.

"Wow," Steve said, slicing into the shriveled bird with his carving knife. "I'm starved."

Dave sat quietly, looking doubtful. Two tapers flickered cheerfully in their silver holders, the smoke from their flames trailing upward to join the thin haze hovering at the ceiling from the oven door that was left open.

He heaped the plates with turkey and potatoes and they sat in silence working at their food, the only sound being that of fork against china.

"France," Steve said, balling his napkin and placing it on the table, "I can't…"

Tears welled up in France's eyes and her lip trembled, but the sight of Steve trying to swallow the piece of turkey that he'd been chewing interminably made her laugh instead.

The two men stared at her, which made her laugh harder.

Steve spit the wad of meat into his napkin and started to say something, but ended up laughing with her. Dave looked from one to the other, not knowing what to say.

"I wanted to tell you that this dinner was as good as my mother's," Steve said when he was finally able to catch his breath. "But I couldn't bring myself to insult her like that!"

France threw her napkin at him. "That was uncalled for! At least I tried."

"Okay, you did. But that still doesn't solve the problem. We need to get food."

"What's open?"

Dave finally spoke. "I think the dining hall is open."

They all got to their feet at the same time and went for their coats.

"France, thanks for…"

"Don't say a thing, Dave," she answered, her hand up to silence him. "I tried to warn you all, but the damn football game had your attention. You just didn't listen."

In early December Steve and France decided to go Christmas shopping. The first wild flurries of snow bit their faces as they walked into the wind. France drew her large pea coat closer, the dark wool scratchy against her neck.

"What do you think about one of those for my parents?" Steve pointed to a display of brass lanterns stacked in the window of a small shop offering nautical items and gifts.

"I think they'd like that. But can we please go get some hot chocolate first? I'm freezing," she said as he pulled her into the store.

"We can get some later, come on. We've got to knock this stuff out before your folks come up next weekend."

A tall blonde woman in a wool turtleneck and plaid skirt approached them.

"France! I've been meaning to call you!"

"Larkin! I'm so glad to see you! Do you work here? Since when?"

"Since today! I just applied for the job yesterday. Completely spur-of-the-moment. I'm only doing it for pocket change."

"What about the twins?"

"Frank is watching them…"

"Oh! Larkin, this is my husband, Steve. Steve, this is my friend Larkin. You know her husband, Frank Mason."

"Larkin, nice to meet you… we were just leaving to grab something to eat. Be sure to say hi to Frank." Steve pulled France toward the door.

"We'll get you guys over for dinner. Nice meeting you, Steve," Larkin called after them.

"Call me later," France called over her shoulder.

"Good Lord, Steve! What was *that* all about? What happened to 'knocking everything out before my folks come?" She yanked her arm away from him.

"I was ready for some hot chocolate, too, that's all," Steve said benignly. "How did you meet her anyway? What's her name…Larkin?"

"I told you…at the meet-and-greet. Do you like Frank?"

"He's kind of a boy scout, if you know what I mean," he said disparagingly. "Not much fun."

"If they ask us to dinner, *I'd* like to go."

"We'll see."

Larkin called the next night. "Why don't you come over for dinner tomorrow night? We're just going to fix a pot roast."

"Hang on, let me ask Steve."

Steve was standing next to her and shook his head vehemently.

"I'm so sorry, Larkin." France shot Steve a dark look. "He's trying to get all his paperwork done before my parents get in this weekend."

"No problem. Let's get together for lunch after they leave. We can try again another time."

"That would be great. I'll call you."

CHAPTER TEN

Francc and Stevc sat on the couch watching television. They could hear the tinny chorus of the New Year's Eve crowd shouting the countdown as the ball began to drop at Time's Square. The television provided the only light in the room. France was wrapped in a blanket, her head on Steve's shoulder.

"Three….two…onc…IIappy Ncw Ycar!" thc sound of noisemakers and shouting buzzed into the room.

Steve absently kissed the top of her head. "Happy New Year, babe."

"Larkin will be disappointed we didn't make it to their party."

"She'll get over it. Tell her you're pregnant or something."

"Why do you say things like that? That's just *rude.*"

Steve pulled on his coat. "I'm going to run over to the "O" Club for a quick beer. A few of the guys are by themselves…"

"Are you kidding? I'll be by myself. Don't go."

"One beer. That's it."

"No! You never stay home with me, and you never take me out, either!"

"That's not true," he answered.

"It is true, Steve. We need to spend more time together. You know we do."

As he turned to leave, she sat up. "Steve! Steve, come back."

"What?"

"Give me your hand." She placed it on her abdomen. "Feel. The baby moved. Can you feel it?""

He withdrew his hand. "I didn't feel anything. Be back in a little."

"Wait, it will happen again…"

"I'll be back later."

She watched him walk out the door, but she was too caught up in the moment to care. She was enthralled. That tiny little stirring, that little flutter deep in her belly, and she was suddenly, deeply connected to the little person batting around in there. She felt it again, although the movement was not quite as strong this time.

Poor, pathetic Steve.

Spring was blustery and cold in Newport. France was picking her way through leftover icy puddles on the sidewalk to meet Larkin for lunch at a little café on the waterfront, avoiding puddles as she walked. She ached to see a Virginia spring. The woods would have punches of vibrant purple from the early redbud, and sprays of yellow forsythia would line the fencerows. She missed the smell of fresh mown fields and the pungent, earthy smell of manure. Breezes in the South were sweet, not savage. She longed to rake her fingers through the loamy soil of her mother's garden.

She skirted a particularly deep puddle, feeling bulky and unwieldy. Two weeks to go. She drew her muffler tighter against the sharp wind. She was looking forward to spending time with Larkin. It would take her mind off her issues with Steve. He was so distant these days. The larger her waistline got, the further away he seemed. He never touched her belly, not even when the baby kicked. She tried so hard to engage him, but he was always preoccupied and testy.

Maybe he's just tired, she thought. He was commuting every day to Mystic, Connecticut, so that they could keep the apartment in Newport until after the baby was born. He never seemed to smile anymore, she thought sadly.

She brightened when she caught a glimpse of Larkin through the window of the café.

"Hey! How long have you been waiting?"

"Not real long. It feels good to have a little quiet time when you have two babies fussing at the same time…"

"I can't even imagine," France breathed, settling into her booth.

"Wow… you look like you're going to go any minute! It looks like you've dropped."

"I hope not. I still have two weeks to go, you know. But, I tell you what, I'm ready. It's hard to even sleep now. I can't seem to find a comfortable position anymore."

"I remember all too well. It's so exciting, though. I swear, I think Frank was more excited than I was…" She could have bitten her tongue. She'd heard the stories. Steve was hardly behaving like an eager young father-to-be.

A cloud passed briefly over France's face, but she said smilingly, "I think Steve is looking forward to the delivery, but he is just exhausted. He's got that commute, and all the studying… he still fits in his afternoon run, and I'm glad he does. It helps him so much…" She had an awful feeling she was saying too much. "I think I'm getting some chocolate cake. Who knows when we'll get back here?"

"Me, too. That sounds great. And France," Larkin reached across the table, patting her on the arm. "Call me anytime, if you need to talk."

Three days later France sat on the edge of the bed, swinging her legs on the side. The day had been fresh and damp, finally hinting at spring.

"So how late are you going to be?" She was trying to be heard over the shower.

Steve shut the water off and emerged, wrapping himself in a towel.

"Did you say something?"

"I said," France couldn't keep the frustration from her voice. "I said, how late are you going to be? How long is this thing supposed to last?"

"I don't know. I haven't been to one before. It's a reward banquet for all the hard work we've put in. I have to go."

"But what if I need to go to the hospital?"

"France. It's April. You're not even close," he said tightly. "Don't try to use your pregnancy to manipulate me."

France was stung. "Manipulate you? If I'd wanted to manipulate you I would have used it every night this week, because that's all you do. You go out and leave me here."

It's called *work*, France. Work. I have to work extra hard, because I have to support a family now."

Her voice was small. "Even at night?"

"Especially at night. All I do is work to provide for you and…" he pointed at her body, "that."

Tears burned her eyes. "How can you say that?"

"Because I didn't sign up for this. Don't you think I'd like to just hang out and watch TV? "

She opened her mouth to say something, but the words wouldn't come.

"So don't start with me. I'm doing the best I can. I'll see you when I see you."

He went into the other room and a few minutes later she heard the door slam.

"Larkin, this is France."

Larkin looked blearily at the alarm clock next to her bed. Three o'clock.

"What is it? Are you okay?"

"No, I don't think so. It *hurts*. I'm having bad pains."

Larkin sat up quickly, now wide awake. "Tell me where you're hurting, honey."

"I don't know," she replied, her voice catching. "Everywhere."

"Okay, how close are your pains?"

"I think every three minutes."

"And how long has this been going on?"

"It started about five hours ago..." France's voice trailed off as another pain gripped her body.

"Tell Steve to take you in. Now." Larkin looked in the direction of her sleeping husband, who had rolled over, taking half the covers with him. She was fully awake now.

"That's why I'm calling… I don't know where he is. He's not back from the banquet."

"He's not back yet? Honey, it's three o'clock."

"I know. I thought he might be with Frank."

I know where he'd better *not* be, Larkin thought. That son-of-a-bitch. "No, sweetie. You know Frank. He dragged himself in at eleven. He could be with Sam or Rob…"

France started to cry.

"Hang in there, France. I'm on my way. Do you have your things ready?"

"No…I didn't think it would start so soon."

"Stay by the door. We'll get your things later. I'll be there in five minutes."

Larkin hung up the phone, pulling her clothes on as she ran. She stopped long enough to kiss Frank.

"I need to take France to the hospital…she's in labor. Don't forget to give the babies their vitamins in the morning." Thank God Frank was off tomorrow.

"Where's Steve?" Frank squinted into the overhead light.

"He didn't quite finish celebrating last night, apparently." Her eyes flashed angrily. "I'll call you in the morning."

The first rosy fingers of daylight were stretching across the gray sky when Steve sprinted to the front door, fumbling for his keys. The air around him was heavy with stale cigarettes and whiskey. He glanced at his watch before turning the key. Six o'clock. He snatched up the morning paper. With any luck, France would still be asleep. He stepped into the darkened living room. The shades were still drawn and the early morning light filtered in behind them. He sat heavily on the couch. The door to the bedroom was partially open. He slid his shoes off one at a time, his mind skimming over the conversation he would have with her when she woke. It was late, didn't want to wake you. I know how difficult it's been for you to sleep…

He adjusted the couch pillow slightly and smiled. He wondered what Sam was saying to his wife right about now.

He jumped as the phone jangled next to him. "Yeah," he whispered thickly. Who the heck would be calling at this hour? Maybe Sam needed a place to stay…

"Steve, this is Larkin Mason."

"Okay?"

"I thought you might want to know that France went to the hospital a few hours ago." Her voice was precise and cold.

"She did? Is…is she all right?" He found himself looking beyond the door, into the bedroom.

"No, Steve, not really. She's having a really tough time, poor little thing, having your baby. She's in a lot of pain. Listen, I've got to go. They're bringing her out of x-ray."

Suddenly, he was clear and alert. "I'll be right there, Larkin. Thanks for calling."

"Right, Steve. No need to hurry. You probably need to rest up." She couldn't help herself.

"I'll be there in two." He hung up the phone. X-ray? Crap. What if something was wrong with the baby? Or France? In his mind he saw the pre-pregnancy France, smiling on the beach, her cheeks flushed. Something not unlike a prayer flitted through his head: please let them make it. Don't let anything go wrong.

France was so grateful to be lying back on the gurney. The ordeal of having to lie rigid on the slanting x-ray board was more than she could bear. She wanted to curl up when another pain rolled over her, but the technicians wouldn't let her. The pains came crashing on top of her and she was forced to lie in a straight position, almost wavering in and out of consciousness with the intensity of it. As it receded her muscles relaxed completely, and she was limp until the next one.

The sunlight from the windows in the hallway seared her eyes and she closed them.

Larkin stood by, smoothing damp tendrils of hair from France's forehead.

"Steve's on his way, France." Her voice was comforting, like Mama's was when France was little and sick in bed. "It won't be long before the baby comes. You're doing great."

A tear squeezed out of France's eye. "It *hurts*, Larkin. It hurts so badly. I want it to stop."

"You're almost there, you're doing fine. I know it hurts. It won't be too much longer." Larkin looked up anxiously to see if she could see a doctor nearby. They need to at least tell us *something*, she thought. Her own labor was painful, but not this rough. France was just so tiny…

At the sound of an approaching male voice, France struggled to sit up, but fell against a thin pillow as another pain took hold. Was that Steve?

Larkin moved out of the way to allow a young resident to talk to France.

"Mrs. Marshall, I'm Dr. White. I'm the obstetrician on call today." He had blue eyes just like Steve's. "Your friend says your husband will be here shortly."

France nodded mutely.

"Mrs. Marshall, we're going to be making some tough decisions in the next thirty minutes. Your labor is not progressing as rapidly as we would like. We do not want your baby to go into distress. We may need to schedule a caesarean section if the baby isn't born within the next half hour. It's safer for you and the baby…do you understand, Mrs. Marshall?"

France nodded weakly. She didn't care anymore. She wanted the baby to be born and the pain to be over. She never dreamed that it was ever going to hurt like this. What had she thought? Maybe some minor discomfort, and then a baby. The baby would be sweet and rosy, and she would be fresh and scrubbed, hair shiny and combed, cuddling the baby.

"Now, would you like something for pain?"

Larkin was nodding yes, but France shook her head no. Larkin shrugged at the doctor.

"I read that it's better for the baby not to have pain meds," she whispered.

"Honey, I think it's better for you that you *do*… what is it?" Larkin hovered over her in consternation.

France suddenly felt herself detaching from the pain, floating away from it, although the pressure of the baby moving down was pulling her back to earth.

"Doctor! Doctor!" Larkin turned quickly to look for the resident. "Something's changed…"

Dr. White stepped toward France, passing his hands over her straining abdomen. Turning to an orderly, he said, "Let's get her back to delivery." He smiled. "Mrs. Marshall, I think you're about to have a baby!"

Stepping off the elevator, Steve headed toward the reception desk on the maternity floor. The heavy-set nurse manning the desk peered at him from a small pair of glasses perched at the end of her nose. She stopped shuffling a stack of papers.

"Do you need something?"

"I'm looking for my wife…Lucy Marshall. Could you please tell me what room she's in?"

"And you're her husband?"

Steve couldn't mask his irritation. "Yes, ma'am, I said my *wife.*"

"I believe she's the little girl in two-twenty-seven. She came in last night." She gave Steve a hard look. "You'll have to scrub and gown before you can go in and see her…I'll be with you in a minute."

Steve lingered, drumming his fingers on the counter.

"Sir, please take a seat. I will be with you momentarily."

Larkin slipped behind him and tapped his shoulder. "When did you get here?"

"Just now. Where is she?"

"She's coming out of delivery now. Any second. Don't you want to know what you got?"

Steve looked blank, then smiled weakly. "Oh, yeah, what was it?"

"*It*," Larkin said, and Steve realized that there was no warmth in her voice or friendliness in her eyes, " is a beautiful little girl. Just like her mama."

"Wow…a girl?" Steve had the appearance of someone trying to absorb a difficult piece of information.

"It's a real shame you missed the show. You would've been real proud of France. She was a real trouper."

The doors opened behind them and a gurney was wheeled out. It wasn't France. Steve looked questioningly at Larkin.

"They're cleaning the baby up. It takes a few minutes," she said coldly.

The doors opened again, and this time it was France, cradling a small, blanketed form.

"Steve," she said, smiling weakly. "You made it."

"Hey, France. Yeah, I'm here."

"S'cuse, me, France. I'm going to leave you two alone. I've got to get home." Larkin refused to look at Steve.

"Larkin, " France turned to her. "Thank you so much. I don't know what I would have done…"

"You did all the work, France. I'm just glad I *could* be there." This time she did look at Steve.

"Look, Steve." France said softly, pulling the blanket back from the little dark-haired, red-faced infant. "A little girl."

"She's beautiful," lied Steve. What else could he say? Red, wrinkled? What did he think the baby would look like? Probably like one of those television babies, pink and sitting up.

"Mr. Marshall". The nurse moved in beside him. "Before you touch your baby, you are going to *have* to scrub up and put a gown on. Now." Turning to France, her voice was kinder. "He'll be right back, once we've cleaned him up."

France settled wearily back into the pillow, savoring the stirrings of the baby next to her. She loved the sense of completeness and the depth of love she was feeling. She placed her finger into the tiny hand and felt the little fingers tighten around it. She stared at the delicate curve of her cheek and the upturned nose and the perfect mouth.

"You're really here," she whispered. Her heart was filled with love for this tiny little being, a feeling she had never held for another person. "I love you so much."

They christened her Anne Talbot Marshall after France's mother, but decided to call her Tally. They held the service at Trinity Episcopal Church in

Newport with both families in attendance. Martha came up with her husband Richard, and Grady came with Steve's parents.

Standing in the doorway of the white-framed church France couldn't remember being so happy. She glanced at Steve, who winked at her. He has really changed, she thought. He acts like a decent husband, all of a sudden.

Tally, wearing the ancient Ridley christening gown worn by Ridley babies since Lord-knows-when, was none too happy when the priest took her in hand and sprinkled holy water in the sign of the cross on her little forehead. She screamed at the top of her lungs.

But she quieted down and was quite sociable afterwards.

"That is the most beautiful baby I have ever seen," commented an older woman known to France only as Mrs. MacDougall.

"She is, isn't she?" Steve said proudly.

"See, darlin'? I told you that everything would work out with a little effort, didn't I?" Her mother patted her gently.

France smiled benignly. "Yes, you did, Mama. You were right." Not even Martha knew how bad things had been. She looked over at Larkin, Tally's new godmother, standing with Frank, the twins in their stroller. Larkin knew, although they really never opened up about it. But France knew that she knew.

She hoped Larkin would know that everything was going to be okay now, because it was.

CHAPTER ELEVEN

Alexandria, Virginia
August 1969

Tally was tucked in her cloth infant seat, batting at her duck mobile, surrounded by packing boxes. France sat on the floor next to her, trying to figure out what crate to open next.

Moving was hard; moving with a baby was harder. She realized with a start that she had accomplished something her mother never did. She had moved. Mama came to 'Clifton' as a bride and the babies that followed only ever knew the old house as home.

"Okay, okay," France said out loud, looking around her. She was thrilled with the new quarters. They were brighter, larger and more spacious, and, best of all, they were in Alexandria, only two hours from Richmond and her beloved farm.

She hated saying good-bye to Larkin. They hugged and laughed at each other for tearing up.

"Well, France. This is it," Larkin said in her throaty voice. "At least you'll be the first to hear our news…"

France pulled away. "News? Go on…"

"Well," Larkin took a deep breath. "Another little Mason is on the way…"

"Oh, my Lord, *Larkin*! That's wonderful! When?" Her face fell. "I won't be here to help *you.*"

"In about seven and a half months. I just got the call from the doc this morning."

"That is just great."

Larkin looked at her watch. "I need to run. It's better this way. I really can't prolong good-byes. They rip me apart."

"Can you wait just a few minutes to say good-bye to Steve?"

Larkin's features hardened. "No. I don't think I have time for that." As quickly as the smile had left her face, it returned. "We'll write. We'll keep in touch. Alexandria is a stone's throw away… really. So, I am not going to say good-bye. I'll say 'see ya later.'"

She stooped to kiss Tally lightly on the forehead and ran out the door.

Sitting in the middle of her living room packed with boxes, France thought about Larkin. Military wives were a tight bunch, she realized. When push came to shove, it was your friends that got you through all the mess.

1974

"Blow, darlin' blow!" Tally was pursing her lips, trying with all her might to blow out the pink candles on her birthday cake. The entire class of five-year-olds surrounded her, shouting encouragement.

"Harder, Tally, harder!"

"You can do it! Blow!"

She blew out three of the candles, but the two remaining candles flickered annoyingly back to life.

"Mommy!" Tally stomped her foot in frustration. "I can't do it."

France smiled. Holy Lord, she looks like me, she thought. She even acts like me.

"You can do it, honey. Try one more time."

"I won't get my wish now."

"Yes, you will. You'll get most of it."

Placated, Tally went back to work.

"You did it!" came the chorus as the last two candles were blown out.

Steve walked in the door at that moment.

"Daddy!" Tally ran toward the door and jumped in his arms.

"Did I miss anything?" he grinned, looking at France.

She smiled back. "Not too much. Tally just blew out all her candles."

Tally beamed.

"Sorry I'm late. The traffic was pretty heavy getting here."

"It's fine. She's so thrilled that you took off work to come. We waited as long as we could."

Steve looks so good, France thought, surveying him from across the room. Every now and again she saw him as others might see him. He was out of the Navy now and working for a small investment company in Washington. They bought a house within walking distance from school. Things were so much better she sometimes felt she needed to pinch herself to make sure she wasn't dreaming. He was so affectionate lately. The surge of passion in their lovemaking was a direct result of that.

She and Steve laughed seeing Tally interact with her classmates. She was such a little corker. France was initially against letting Tally go to kindergarten; she was only just turning five. But she was precocious and loved learning and here, in Mrs. Johansson's classroom, there was no doubt that this was the best choice for their daughter.

During the day while Tally was at school was another story. France felt at loose ends with herself. She had her friends and her routine, but there was something missing. She remembered a short lecture given her by her father the day before her wedding. It was about developing "marketable skills." She didn't have any. The paralegal course was a thing of the past. She'd given that up when she married. But, what to do?

She was in her garden when it hit her. She was kneeling in the grass, preparing to plant a flat of perennials. The soil was turned and ready and the air around her was redolent with the smells of fresh grass and loam and she realized, with the clarity of being struck by a lightning bolt, what it was that she was happiest doing: gardening. She stuck her spade in the ground, pulled off her gloves and raced inside to make a phone call.

That night at dinner, breathless with excitement, she made her announcement.

"I have to tell you what I decided to do today."

Steve looked up from putting his napkin in his lap.

"I am going to take courses in landscape design and horticulture."

"You're what?" Steve asked in surprise. "What made you do that?"

Her fork dropped. "What made me *do* it? Have you not been listening to me at all? I want to be productive… I want to do something fulfilling while Tally is at school. As Daddy always said, I need a marketable skill. That's what *made* me do it."

"Whoa! You don't have to get your back up…"

"Yes, I do. I could use some encouragement."

"Hey. I'm not against you going back to school. But why don't you think about teaching or something? Why would you want to dig around in the dirt when you could do something better with your life?"

She struggled for words. "Are you kidding me? Do you not know me at all?"

Steve's mouth was set in irritation. "Look, I've had a hard day." He glanced at Tally, who was dragging her fork through her mashed potatoes. "We can take this up later."

France drummed her fingers on the table, trying to figure out what to say. "There's really nothing to 'take up later,' Steve. I've signed up for classes. It's what I want to do. I don't want to teach. I don't want to be a nurse. I grew up on a farm, I love being outside, and I am creative."

His eyes were hard, challenging. "Well, since you've made your mind up…I won't try to stop you."

"Wow, thank you." Her voice was dripping with sarcasm. "That just means the world to me, knowing that you won't try to stop me."

Steve glared, turning sharply to Tally. "Stop playing with your food!"

Tally's eyes filled with tears.

"Good Lord, what has gotten into you? I signed up for a few classes and you turn on Tally?"

The sound of Steve's chair scraping on the bare wood floor filled the room.

He balled his napkin up and shoved it onto his plate.

"I'm getting out of here." He stood tall, looming over them.

"When will you be back?" France shrank back imperceptibly.

"No telling!"

She and Tally watched him, mouths open, as he walked toward the door, slamming it shut behind him.

CHAPTER TWELVE

"Step on a crack, you break your mother's back!" Tally sang as she jumped over the deep lines of the sidewalk on the way to school. The leaves were just starting to turn and there was a crisp bite to the air. Their footsteps resounded in the dry leaves.

"Be careful with those cracks, girlie," France called after her. "I need my back to be in good shape for my classes."

Tally stopped in the middle of a square. "Don't worry, I'm always careful."

"That's one of the many reasons Mommy loves you, precious."

"Mommy," Tally said thoughtfully. "Do you think it's weird that you're a mommy and you're in school?" She had trouble with the word weird. She gave it two syllables: *wee-uhd.*

"Not at all, darlin'. Just because you grow up doesn't mean you stop wanting to learn things. Grown-ups like school, too. Besides," she added, "Mommy wants to have a good job someday."

Tally wheeled around. "But why? Daddy works."

"Yes, he does, honey. Daddy works hard. But now that you're in school, Mommy wants to do something, too."

"Oh." Tally digested the information. "Mommy, doesn't that smoke smell like the farm?"

France stopped, filling her lungs with the scent of aromatic wood smoke curling up from the chimney of a nearby house.

"It does. It smells exactly like the farm."

"I want to go to 'Clifton'. Why don't we go anymore?"

"We'll go for Thanksgiving, you know that."

"It's not enough. I miss Grannah and Big Daddy."

"They miss you, too, honey. They miss you so much. We do need to go soon. I miss it as much as you do."

"Mommy, did Grannah and Big Daddy fight when you were a little girl?"

She has to ask the hard questions, thought France. "They never really fought. They didn't always agree on everything, but they…worked it out."

"Why don't you and Daddy work it out?"

"Well, we do," France replied.

"But you fight. I *hear* you."

"We do. But it doesn't mean we don't love each other. Mamas and daddies can disagree… just about everyone can disagree…"

"But Big Daddy and Grannah love each other and they don't fight."

I wish someone had told me that being a mother would be this tough, she thought as she stopped, pulling Tally to her.

Squaring Tally's shoulders with her hands, she looked into the child's eyes. "Different people have different ways of handling their differences. Grannah and Big Daddy talked through their issues. Mama and Daddy argue- we don't fight, we argue. But at the end of the day, we all love each other, and everyone loves *you*. Okay?"

Tally nodded solemnly. "Okay."

"Now go get your little patootie to school. Did you remember your lunch money?"

Tally held it up.

"Love you, bootnin' bug."

"Love you, too, Mommy."

France loved her classes. As soon as she deposited Tally in Mrs. Logan's first grade class, she trotted home to hop in her car and drive to school. She loved it all; the practicum, the homework, even the weight of the notebooks and textbooks she carried under her arm. She felt so energized and alive. Already she broadened her sphere of friends. Many of the people in her classes were older people, seeking to get their degrees after a career. But quite a few were young mothers like her, with the same demands and challenges she faced at home.

"It's not that I'm not fulfilled in my home life," she was saying to Lynne, a blonde with three children, who reminded her of Larkin. Lynne was four years older, and had her hair cut in the new "shag" hairstyle, a look that was popping up all over campus.

"No, I understand, trust me. When Charlie was born all I wanted to do was stay home and hold him. Nothing else! You know that feeling, don't you?"

France nodded.

"I mean, Charlie was my third child...I know how quickly it flies by. But now that he's in second grade..."

"It's probably a little bit more than that for me," France said reflectively. "Steve is out of the military and is busy working for a company that involves a lot of travel. There's no time for me. None whatsoever. He does see Tally late at night. She stays awake so that he can tuck her in bed."

"That's sad," Lynne said. "What do you all do together?"

"Precious little. Oh, I do the corporate wife thing from time… but I feel like I'm being kept in a box and Steve takes me out whenever he needs me."

Lynne shook her head in disbelief. "I can't imagine feeling like that."

"Really?"

"I've never been made to feel that way. But, then again, I'm not a corporate wife, either."

"What does your husband do?"

"He's a teacher. He teaches English at Fort Hunt High School. And he's been great with the kids. I'm not sure I could handle the workload if he didn't help out as much as he does."

"Well, you've got three kids…I've only got one. But I feel like I'm leading a dual life."

"What do you mean?"

France shrugged. "Well, here I wear jeans and tee shirts and I hang out with all you radicals…"

Lynne laughed. "Okay. Berkley East. Got it."

"Okay, hear me out. But I go home to a husband in a business suit and when we go out, I'm in heels and a dress, and I either go to dinner parties or I throw one."

"Which life is the best fit then?"

France furrowed her brow. "Right now, this one. I like myself best when I'm here. Wait, I didn't mean that." She paused. "I guess what I'm trying to say, is that I feel more like who I really am, being here, in jeans and a tee shirt. When I'm with Steve I feel like I'm play-acting, like a child playing dress-up."

Lynne started to say something, then stopped.

"What?" France looked at her quizzically.

"Do you and Steve ever just have fun? A relaxed weekend?"

France sighed. "Lynne, he's gone all the time. He goes to California, sometimes twice a month. He gets home in time to kiss Tally goodnight. He spends most nights in his study, prepping for his next meeting. So, to answer your question, we don't really have fun. I'm not even sure what fun looks like anymore."

"It sounds like Steve needs to loosen up." Lynne's face brightened. "You know, we socialize with a bunch of teachers from Ft. Hunt… we have the best time. We have barbecues and touch football games and we play softball. We play cards in the winter. I'll let you know the next time we do something. Maybe we can get Steve to lose the tie and to learn to play a little bit." She smiled.

"Yeah, we'd love that," France said doubtfully. Somehow she couldn't picture Steve at a party with a fun group of teachers. "Let me know."

She tried to remember the last time she and Steve had gone out, just to have fun. She couldn't even think of the last time… Ever since their fight, Steve had been less affectionate, and a lot more withdrawn.

Wow, she thought. Things can turn on a dime, can't they? We were doing so well, and now we're not. We really do need to learn to have fun together... not everything needs to revolve around business and children. She looked up at Lynne and smiled gamely. She wondered if Lynne ever wondered from day to day whether she was going to feel happy in her marriage.

CHAPTER THIRTEEN

June 1976

As the graduates took their seats on that sweltering June day, they resembled a huge flock of shiny crows in their black caps and gowns. France shifted uncomfortably on her gray metal folding chair. Her gown stuck to the back of her legs, like a pancake frying on a griddle. Sweat trickled down the backs of her knees.

She twisted in her chair trying to find her family in the crowd. Her eyes skimmed the sea of faces and alit on the chiseled features of her father. Catching his eye, she smiled. He smiled back and leaned down, pulling Tally onto his lap, pointing in France's direction. Tally waved excitedly, nestling back into her grandfather's lap, smoothing the folds of her crisp pink dress with her small brown hands.

Where was Steve? France strained to see if she could see him making his way across the perimeter of the green. She turned back to face the stage. From the next aisle, Lynne waved her hand. Where's your husband? she mouthed.

Not here yet, she mouthed back. Lynne nodded sympathetically.

She hardly listened to the speeches. This is so surreal, she thought. Graduations are so formulaic. This really didn't feel much different from her graduation from high school, except this time there was a little girl in a pink dress in the audience who was her responsibility. I did it! she thought. For the first time, she allowed herself to feel elated. *I* have a marketable skill.

Her thoughts were interrupted by her row getting to their feet. They moved toward the stage like so many cattle being herded. The act of moving cooled the sticky dampness of her skin.

"Lucy Frances Ridley Marshall," droned the president of the school at the podium.

She walked decorously across the stage looking in the direction of her family, but was blinded by the pop of flash bulbs coming from that direction.

When it was all over, she wove through the crowd to find them.

"Mommy!"

She made her way toward Tally's voice.

"Hey! Well, I did it!"

"Yes, you did, darlin'," her mother said, beaming.

"I'm proud of you, honey," Daddy said.

She hugged him. "I didn't forget our talk, Daddy."

"What talk? What did Big Daddy say?" Tally piped up.

She stooped down to the little girl's eye level. "Big Daddy told me, before I married your daddy," she paused, looking up at her parents. "Who, by the way, doesn't seem to be here," she struggled to keep the giveaway hard edge out of her voice.

Tally interrupted. "Grannah said he's probably stuck in traffic."

"I'm sure that's what happened. Bad traffic always seems to find your daddy. Anyway, Big Daddy said it's important to go to school and get a degree, just in case."

"Just in case what?"

"Just in case," she stopped to choose her words. "In case I ever want to get a job. And I do. In fact, Tally, I have a job. I'm going to work at Miss Bernadette's."

"Honey, that's wonderful!" Her mother patted her shoulder.

"I was going to make the announcement at dinner, but now was as good a time as any to tell ya'll the news."

"*Miss Bernadette's?*" Tally tugged on her gown. "That big fat lady with the plumpy cheeks and the curly hair and all the plants?"

France looked shocked. "Tally, that's not nice. Besides, you like Miss Bernadette... and she likes you."

"I don't like her."

"Yes, you do. You said she was nice to you."

"But she's still big with plumpy cheeks."

France looked helplessly at her mother.

"When do you start, dear?" Her mother smiled evenly.

"Actually, I start next week."

"Next week? Who's going to take care of me?" Tally looked wildly between her mother and her grandparents.

France smoothed Tally's hair. "I can work around your school schedule. You won't even know I'm working, bug. It'll be fine...you'll see."

After lunch, France walked her parents to their car.

"When does Steve go out of town again?" her mother asked.

A soft breeze brought a refreshing respite from the hot sun.

"Week after next."

"Why don't you and Tally come to the farm for a bit while he's gone."

"We'd love to… we could make a long weekend of it. Bernadette doesn't have me working weekends, that I know of."

Her mother squeezed her hand, looking at her meaningfully. "Wonderful. I think it would do everyone a world of good."

Steve's car pulled into the driveway at seven.

Time to face the lion's den, he thought. "Hey, everyone!" he called, walking through the door. His voice sounded stiffly cheerful.

"Daddy!" Tally squealed, throwing herself into his arms.

"Hey, pumpkin," he said, picking his daughter up. "How did the ceremony go? Sorry I couldn't make it. His tone was breezy, light. "The meetings ran on… they added an extra one…"

France said nothing. She looked at him bitterly. Steve ignored her.

"Grannah said you were stuck in traffic," offered Tally.

"That Grannah is a smart lady. I almost was stuck in traffic."

"Mommy has a job."

Steve looked surprised. "You do? Already? Well, good for you. Who with?"

"She's going to work for Miss Bernadette."

Steve's mouth dropped open. "You're working for Bernadette? That huge woman with the curly hair?"

France's eyes blazed. "For the love of God," she said tightly, and stormed out of the house, slamming the door behind her.

Steve sighed. He felt a twinge of guilt. He probably could have cancelled the last meeting…but he didn't feel like missing work to sit through a graduation ceremony. It's just an associate's degree, he thought to himself. Not like she's gone and gotten her PhD. He wondered if his in-laws would be critical. No, he didn't think so. They seemed to try hard to keep things steady.

"Okay, Tally, time for bed."

"No! Not yet! Daddy, it's only seven-thirty."

Steve looked at his watch in surprise. "You're right. Have you had dinner yet?"

"I'm not hungry."

"Where do you suppose your mama went?"

Tally's eyes were dark and worried. "I don't know. Maybe she went to the store?" she said hopefully, adding, "I don't think she likes you to talk mean about Miss Bernadette. She's mad at you."

Steve smiled, messing up Tally's hair. "That wasn't very nice of me, was it?"

"I said she was big, just like you did," Tally whispered. "She's probably mad at me, too."

The clouds in the distance were roiling, dark, and threatening, and France pointed her car straight into them. The air turned green around her and still she drove on, even as the rain battered down on her car, so heavy the windshield wipers couldn't push the sheets of water away from her windshield fast enough. She drove until the visibility was so poor that she was forced to pull over. She pulled under an overpass, and sat, listening to the rubbery scratching of the wipers against the now-dry windshield. She didn't even know where she was. Up ahead she could see a stoplight dancing crazily in the high winds, the lamps watery green, yellow and red, bouncing orbs in the thick rain.

The anger had left her a while ago. Achiness and fatigue had taken its place.

What was wrong with her and what was wrong with Steve? I don't know him, she thought. He doesn't know me.

He didn't know what made her happy or what her dreams were. Oh, yeah, he knew how she took her coffee in the morning, but that was about it. If you pay attention at all, you're bound to pick up something. He didn't know that fall was her favorite time of year, and that the smell of old brick and boxwood almost made her cry with nostalgia. He didn't know that she loved being a mother and wanted whatever it was her mother and father shared between them in their marriage. He didn't touch her, or hold her, or joke with her. He got up, went to work, came home. He spent time with Tally; he was a good father, she would give him that. He didn't even really smile anymore. If he did, it was when he might be talking to Charlie on the phone. And, thinking of Charlie, what was with all the trips to California?

As she sat there in the car on that summer night she realized that she didn't know what Steve's dreams and hopes for the future were, either. She didn't know Steve. He was a total stranger. And she had shared his bed for eight years.

Oh, my Lord, she thought. Oh, my Lord.

Fall was in full force before she finally got to the farm. The trees were burnished in brilliant reds and golds and the surrounding fields were golden and brown.

She stepped from her car, filling her lungs with the crisp air and wood smoke. It was an unusually chilly day, with the promise of the first frost around the corner.

"Hey, Mama," she called as her mother came down the walkway.

"Grannah!" Tally hurtled herself toward her grandmother.

"Four months!" remonstrated her mother.

"I know, I know," France apologized. "How was I to know that Bernadette would have me working around the clock? Honestly," she held her hands up. "I was lucky to get away for an overnight."

"She works all the time, Grannah," Tally pouted.

"Well, you're both here, and that's all that matters," Mrs. Ridley said briskly. "Come in, I've made my famous apple cider and, looking at Tally, " molasses sugar cookies, your favorite. Then, if you two city girls can keep up with me, we'll go for a walk."

"I am so glad to be home, Mama. I can't tell you how homesick I've been."

"Your daddy will be so glad to see you, honey. I think he takes it harder than me when you can't come home."

The walk was long and invigorating. Their cheeks burned bright from the sharp air. Tally was running ahead of them down the long lane to the house, laughing from the sheer joy of being able to run without having to stop to cross a street.

"I remember doing that same thing," France smiled.

"I remember you doing that, too, answered her mother. "I declare, she is you made over."

"She is, isn't she?"

"What time are you picking up Steve at the airport?"

"I don't have to pick him up. He drove his car."

"Can you stay another day, then?"

"No, Mama, I really can't. I need to get Tally settled down for school on Monday…I wish I could." Their footsteps stirred the fallen dry leaves as they walked. "Is Daddy okay? He seemed tired this weekend…"

"He's moving a bit more slowly these days…" her mother replied. "It's probably old age more than anything."

France stopped in her path. "It's not like him not to join us for a walk… he loves the outdoors."

"Has he mentioned that he's thinking of selling the practice?"

"What?" France looked at her in concern. "Now I'm really worried. He always said that he'd work 'til he's planted!"

"Yes, he did say that. He's always said that," her mother laughed softly. "He's changed his tune a little bit now, though. He's seventy-two…he always said that if he hadn't gone into law he would've gone into farming."

"…like Granddaddy…"

"…like your Granddaddy. Some lawyers from Tidewater have made him an offer…he hasn't told them anything definite… we'll see what he does."

"Oh, Mama." France took her mother's arm. "I hate change. I do. Why can't things just stay the same? With Daddy going into the office every day, just like always." She couldn't picture a day that wouldn't see her father making the trip to his old book-lined office on Cary Street in Richmond. He was the last of the old school attorneys. "And the farm, with you and Daddy here, always." Her eyes filled with tears.

Her mother hugged her close. "You're a farm girl, born and bred. You know, better than most, the cycle of life."

"I know. But it still doesn't make it any more tolerable."

"No," her mother said thoughtfully. "But it makes you appreciate what you have a little bit more, doesn't it?"

"I expect so."

"You know it doesn't help to have your daddy worry about you…"

"About me? Why would he worry about me?"

"Lord have mercy, France, we're not blind. It doesn't take much to see that you and Steve may not….be doing all that well."

France faltered. "What makes you think that?"

"Well, for one thing, we hear more about Bernadette than we do Steve. We haven't seen him in…" She paused, cocking her head to one side. "Why, I can't think how long it's been."

"Well, he travels a lot," she answered uncomfortably. "And it's not like you and Daddy. I mean, I remember you all sitting in the front room after dinner just sharing your day…Steve and I never do that. He goes straight to his room and doesn't say two words to me. He plays with Tally… he reads to her, if it's not too late when he gets in…" Her voice trailed. "But if I didn't have my job and Tally, I think I'd go crazy."

"Would it help if you had some time alone together? Why don't you go to California with him next time he goes? We can keep Tally."

"It's going to take more than a trip to fix us," France said doubtfully.

"You've got to start somewhere, honey." Her mother was firm. "Daddy and I loved those evenings talking together, but it was more than that. We were building our strong marriage by doing it. If your marriage gets too far away from you, it can be hard to fix it."

"Do you remember Charlie? Steve's best man at our wedding?"

Her mother nodded.

"He's in California. Steve stays with him when he's out there on business. Anyway, he's getting married next month. Steve is in the wedding, but I didn't think I could go, because of Tally…"

"You need to go. We love having Tally here. You know that. You should have asked."

"I'll ask. No, I mean, I'll go. You're right. I know you're right. We need to work on this." She tried hard to make her voice sound resolute. Deep inside she tried to ignore the feeling that gnawed away at her: *There's nothing you can do. You're wasting your time.* And worse: *Steve doesn't want you to go.*

Charlie leaned in the cab window, pounding Steve one more time on the arm.

"Get here the night before, you hear me?"

"You don't need to keep saying that. I'll be there. I'll need to get back at you for the stunts you pulled at …" He started to say, *my wedding,* but thought better of it. "When you stood in for me."

"Right." Charlie's face became somber. "Man, I hope this goes better for me than it did for you."

"You're full of crap. I've got the best of everything."

"See you in three weeks."

The cab pulled off and Steve relaxed into his seat. Charlie's words bothered him. Who was he to go all moral on him? Charlie was wild as a buck. He hadn't earned the nickname Wild Man for nothing. I don't see Charlie settling down that much, he thought. No way. Robin was a good girl, though. Uninhibited, Charlie's type. If anyone could tame Charlie, it would be her. But Charlie wasn't married yet, either. I give it three years before Charlie strays. Three years maximum.

The cab picked up speed, winding in and out of heavy traffic. I love this life out here, thought Steve. The sun was even brighter. And the *women*…oh, dear God. Lana, Robin's friend…a perfect example of a California girl. Long-legged, sun-bleached hair, tan…He was lost in his reverie, when an image of Tally popped in his head. Tiny little Tally, with her golden skin, flashing dark eyes and glossy hair. She was the one good thing about his marriage. Tally. He smiled, thinking of her running at him, jumping into his arms, so happy to see him. He stirred uncomfortably, pricked by the tiniest flicker of guilt. Three more weeks and he'd be back.

CHAPTER FOURTEEN

San Francisco

France sighed loudly, dangling her legs as she sat on the bed in their hotel room. Mama had been to the doctor before she left for San Francisco for some tests. Mama, with her usual strength and pluck, had dismissed any concerns sent her way.

"I'm *fine*," she said steadfastly, as though willing it to be so.

But still France worried. Mama looked so pale when she dropped Tally off. Her energy seemed low.

Steve was taking the world's longest shower and she started when she heard the water shut off. He'd been sick all night after dragging in at four in the morning from Charlie's bachelor party, having left her alone her first night in California. She heard him retching in the bathroom until five and she grappled with the impulse to either let him suffer or play the dutiful wife and hold his head over the commode. Letting him suffer won out and when he at last stumbled to bed and started snoring, she was glad she hadn't helped him. Sleep was destroyed for her, and she lay there deep in the downy pillows and comforters, replaying their conversations over and over in her head.

"If you tag along..." Tag along? She thought. Tag along suggested an unwanted sibling included in an outing uninvited. The more those words bounced back at her, the angrier she became. Why couldn't she have gotten angrier then? "If you tag along, what will we do with Tally?"

"Mama and Daddy want her to stay with them."

"We can't really afford the extra ticket. Not until I close that deal I've been working on."

"They said they would pay for mine." Wow, she thought. They really must be worried about my marriage.

"Well, then...no more discussion. Come along." Steve's voice was anything but enthusiastic. She looked past it.

And here she was. Steve turned over, flipping his arm leadenly over her pillow, almost hitting her, prompting her to rise. She had stood at their window, watching the heavy mist rolling over the Bay, blanketing the glittering city in fog.

Steve finally emerged from the shower, hair dripping, a towel at his waist. He nodded in her direction.

"Feeling better?" She tried to sound chipper and sincere, but a small amount of bitterness leaked into her words.

He shrugged his shoulders. "I guess."

"What time should we leave?"

"I have to leave at eleven. You can leave at one if you want."

"I want to leave whenever you leave. Let's go together…"

"Okay, whatever, then we're leaving at eleven."

France fought back the hurt that threatened to take over her body.

"It's ten-fifteen. I guess I'd better get dressed."

She pulled her dress out of the hanging bag in the closet. What to wear to a beach wedding in California? When she chose the dress in Virginia, she felt confident. It was a crisp navy blue tea length, acceptable for just about any dressy occasion. She had no idea what would go out here. She guessed she was about to find out. She realized the thought hadn't crossed her mind to ask Steve what he was wearing. She assumed the Virginia uniform: khaki pants, button-down collar shirt, nice tie, blue blazer.

Slipping the dress over her head, she surveyed herself in the mirror, smoothing her hair into place.

She was surprised how grown-up she looked. She looked like a woman who might have a six-year-old child.

She stepped toward Steve.

"How do I look?" she asked in a small voice.

"Fine," he answered without looking up.

"Do we have time to grab lunch and sightsee a little before we go to the wedding?"

"I can't eat, and you can do all that before we fly out tomorrow."

Don't complain, she thought to herself. She looked around for something to occupy herself with; she picked up the San Francisco Examiner that was left at their door this morning.

Steve walked out wearing a white linen shirt and khaki pants.

"Time to go."

"Is that what you're wearing?" She was caught off guard by his apparel.

"No, France, I'm not wearing this. I just put it on so you would ask about it. What do you think?"

"I didn't know," she faltered. "It's just…different from what you usually wear, that's all. It's really casual."

"This is California. Virginia is more uptight. Our cab is here. Come on."

She took in as much of the scenery as she could on their way to the Presidio, where the wedding would take place. She caught a glimpse of the Golden Gate Bridge, and was thrilled at the steep hills and the trolley cars that pulled those hills. The beach had a wonderful view of the Bridge. France found herself following large groups of people through low-lying thickets of sea grass to the wedding site. It was then she felt overdressed. Everywhere she looked women were dressed in flowing cotton or linen dresses, some with wooden beads sewn on them. No one wore shoes. Everyone seemed tan and long-haired and blonde… even the men.

Holy Lord, she thought, distressed. I look matronly. She felt so *prim*. Her own wedding had been a beach wedding, and everyone still dressed up. It was nothing like this.

She smiled at a man with friendly brown eyes who looked to be about her age, but his skin was already so weathered and sun-damaged it was like parchment.

The mist had already burned off the Bay and the sky was preternaturally blue. A boy of about eighteen started to strum a guitar and a man in a linen shirt and rolled-up pants strolled to the center of the group. France realized that he must be the minister.

As the music got stronger Charlie and Steve came over the crest of the dunes talking companionably. Charlie's hair was curling around his ears and was almost shoulder-length. Even Steve hadn't been as religious about getting his hair trimmed lately, although she never said anything about it to him.

She pursed her lips together. I am on another planet, she kept thinking. Virginia-style is definitely not California-style, not in any way, shape or form. The music changed tempo and Charlie's bride came from the opposite direction, flanked by her maid of honor.

The bride wore a flowing white peasant dress beaded with a few seed pearls at the bodice. Her hair hung down her back. Her face was flushed and bright, and Charlie beamed when he saw her approach.

The maid of honor was a stunning beauty; she reminded France of a medieval painting, with her almond-shaped eyes, small mouth and unadorned light brown hair cascading to her waist. She was wearing a pale rose peasant dress and carried a small basket filled with pinks and verbena.

The ceremony began with short speeches written by the bride and groom, promising to love one another while allowing the other the freedom to be who they were, and ended with the minister pronouncing them husband and wife, friends, lovers and soul mates.

Coolers and picnic baskets were hauled onto the beach and a plank table was set up and loaded with food. It all seemed so unstudied and natural. Clusters of guests pulled up small beach chairs, talking and eating off of paper plates.

Wine and champagne were flowing freely and more than a few people left to go to their cars, returning and smelling suspiciously of smoke. France suspected they were probably smoking marijuana, although she wasn't sure what it smelled like.

Robin and Charlie were sitting side by side on two canvas beach chairs while everyone made toasts. Steve's best man's speech was next.

He stepped up and faced the crowd, champagne glass aloft.

"I've known this guy my whole life…" he began, clearly enjoying himself. "And, for those of us from the *best* coast…."

"Wait a minute!" Someone shouted good-naturedly from the side.

"Oh, sorry," he went on. "None of us ever thought we'd live to see the day that Charlie Watkins would opt out of the smorgasbord of women that always seemed to define his bachelor life…"

"Here, here!" Several of Charlie's friends raised their glasses.

"So we knew that it would take someone mighty incredible to tame old Wild Man…Robin, baby, you're the girl. To Robin…" everyone held their glasses up. "To Robin!"

'…and Wild Man!" "To Wild Man!" Everyone shouted and clinked glasses, laughing and sharing stories.

France settled back in her beach chair absorbing the moment. She watched as Steve moved over toward the stunning maid of honor, leaning in and whispering to her. The girl looked him long in the eyes and nodded. Startled, she felt someone gently tap her shoulder.

"France?"

"Yes?"

It was Robin, Charlie's bride.

"Oh, hi!" She smiled, still trying to watch Steve.

"I just wanted to meet you," Robin said sweetly. "Charlie and I have a little time before we fly to Mexico tomorrow, and wanted to know if you have time to meet us for lunch."

"I know we would love to, but…" she saw Steve squeeze the girl's hand earnestly. "But our flight leaves at eleven. We probably need to be at the airport by ten…"

"Oh, that's a shame." Robin sounded genuinely disappointed.

"Do you think you all might get back east anytime? We have plenty of room…"

"Who's coming back east?" Steve asked as he pulled up a chair beside her.

"Charlie and I were saying last week that we need to make the trip. Who knows? He hasn't seen his parents in a few years. We'll try…"

"Well, you're welcome any old time," France offered warmly.

When Robin left, France turned to Steve and asked pointedly, "So. How do you know her?"

"Who?" Steve answered distractedly.

"What do you mean, *who*? Her. The maid of honor. You seem to know her is all."

"I don't know what you're talking about."

"Steve, I saw you talking to her. How do you know her?"

"Are you serious? She was in the damn wedding. How else do you think I would know her?"

"What were ya'll talking about?"

"Let me set you straight. You are not going to grill me every time I say something to somebody." His jaw clenched. "Do you hear me?"

France looked away, fighting the sudden urge to cry.

Steve got up roughly, almost knocking his chair backward. He walked toward a group of men, and France saw them all laugh about something, making jokes. No one would have guessed that Steve was angry about anything.

The next morning she was looking at the wisps of swirling white clouds and green forests and brown fields underneath the plane, looking like all the topography maps she used to study in her school days. There had been no time to see San Francisco before they went to the airport. Her head was resting against the window; Steve was thumbing through a magazine. They didn't speak. He glanced up briefly as she sighed.

Her parents were waiting for them at the airport with Tally jumping up and down beside them.

"There they are! I see them!" France could hear Tally's high-pitched voice above all the din.

"Hey! How's my girl?" Steve scooped Tally in the air over his head.

Mama and Daddy were smiling, but she could see the questions in their eyes. She smiled back at them, but shook her head slightly to signal that the trip wasn't the success they had hoped it would be.

But still…there was something else.

"What's wrong?" she asked them. Steve was talking to Tally, out of earshot.

"Nothing, honey. Nothing that won't keep 'til later," her mother whispered.

France wouldn't be dissuaded. "Something is not right. What is it?"

"My tests came back, darlin'."

France's heart jumped in her chest. "And?"

"It's cancer. I have breast cancer. But you are not to worry. I'll be fine."

CHAPTER FIFTEEN

December

France sat at her desk, surrounded by work orders speared on small holders. She massaged her throbbing temples with her fingertips. There was a huge order in front of her for wreaths and door swags.

She sat back in her chair, inhaling the wonderful combined smell of cedar, juniper, boxwood and holly. A small fire glowed in the belly of the old woodstove in the corner and a light covering of early snow gleamed pearly gray outside her window.

The sleigh bells hanging on the heavy door jangled as Bernadette breezed through the doorway.

"Hey, Bernadette," she said, trying to keep the weariness out of her greeting. "Is it freezing out there?"

"Not too bad," Bernadette answered in her booming voice. As long as she had lived in the South- twenty-five years by her own reckoning- she had never lost the broad accent of her beloved New England. "You Virginia people are soft! None of you would be able to cut it during a *real* winter!"

France laughed. "Probably not," she conceded. "Our pretend winters are about all we can take."

Bernadette was a heavy, stocky, disheveled woman of about fifty, with frizzy, graying hair she unsuccessfully tried to contain in a wild ponytail. She was outfitted in layers of long johns, blue jeans, flannel shirts and scarves, with heavy woolen socks peeking out of the tops of her sturdy work boots.

"I expect we would weather the cold a little better," France went on, eyeing Bernadette's clothing. "If we could teach ourselves to dress the way you do."

"You'd better believe it," Bernadette chuckled. "Now, what was I going to say?" She furrowed her brow.

Typical Bernadette, thought France. Always going a mile a minute.

"Oh, yeah. We're getting real low on cedar and box. You're going to have to call Cedar Grove and see if they can get us twelve or more cartons of it. We need it yesterday!"

"I thought we had enough…" France said.

"We did, but we just pulled fourteen more orders while you were at lunch."

"We did? Oh my Lord...I didn't see anything on that..."

"That's because I haven't had the time to put it in front of you."

"Oh..."

"I *told* you we'd be busy at Christmas."

"Yes. Yes, you did," France agreed. "I guess I had no idea how busy..."

"Well, you just hold onto your hat. We'll get 'er done. But you need to call Cedar Grove. We're only as quick as our suppliers."

France groaned inwardly. There was so much to learn.

"The number is in the Rolodex by the phone." Bernadette continued.

France moved pieces of rough green Styrofoam and florist tape to find the file buried beneath. She flipped through the ink-stained cards.

"It's not in here, Bee..."

"Try the other side of the phone... I may have left it there when I placed the last order."

She found it underneath the telephone, an ancient coffee stain having left a watery brown ring on the lower right-hand corner.

"Found it! It says 'Walker, Hunter, Cedar Grove Farm…"

"That's it."

"You know you would've had that card in the 'W' section of the Rolodex, Bee. I wouldn't have found it even if it had been put away."

"You'll get it eventually. You're a quick learner…" Bernadette harrumphed.

France tapped her foot impatiently, waiting for someone to pick up. She glanced at the clock. It was already after four.

"Cedar Grove," answered the gravelly male voice on the line. It was the kind of voice that could have belonged to a fifteen year old or an eighty year old.

"Um…Mr Walker? Or is it Mr. Hunter?"

"Either one and you'd be right."

France looked at all those orders on her desk. She didn't have time for games.

"This is France Marshall at Bernadette's…" she kept her response crisp and professional.

"Well, hi. How is old Bernadette?" The voice became warm and friendly.

" 'Old Bernadette' is doing very well, thank you. She asked me to tell you that we need at least twelve more crates of cedar and box immediately, and more if you have it."

"Hold on one second…"

She could hear footsteps recede away from the phone.

"Come on, come *on*…" she drummed her fingers on the table.

The footsteps returned.

"Okay…we have six boxes on the truck. I can get the rest to you by Friday. Would fifteen boxes tide her over?"

"Hold, please…" She muffled the receiver. "Bee, he's only got six boxes. We can get the rest by Friday. He can get us fifteen, total."

Bernadette looked up from the pine roping she was binding together. "Tell him that will work. We'll figure it out. We'll just have to push back those last seven orders. No other way around it."

"She said that will work, Mr…" France said into the receiver.

"It's Hunter Walker."

"Mr. Walker."

"All right, then. I can try to get there before five."

"Thank you. We'll look for you." She hung up the phone. "Great God Almighty, Bee. Can we use anybody else?"

The older woman looked over at her, perplexed. "No, we can't. He's got the freshest and prettiest greenery in town. What's your problem?"

"I don't know." France looked out the window at the long shadows stretching across the yard. "He's slow as molasses in January."

"He's reliable as clockwork. That's worth its weight in gold, especially in this business. Hang around here long enough and you'll appreciate the Hunter Walkers of the world."

By the time the clock hit 6:45 p.m. France became unglued.

"Reliable, my fanny," she said out loud. She was so angry she couldn't see straight.

Why had she agreed to wait for him? She had promised to get home early to hear Tally practice her lines for the school pageant. Bee *would* have to go all the way out to Dumfries this afternoon. Where the hell was Mr. Walker?

At seven she called home.

"It's Mommy!" shouted Tally into the phone. "Are you coming?"

"I can't leave just yet, honey. I have to wait on a delivery. But as soon as it comes…"

"Oh," Tally's voice deflated. "We ate dinner. Daddy ordered pizza."

France worked at being cheerful. "Well, you like that, don't you, darlin'? You love pizza."

"Yeah, I do." France heard Steve in the background, reminding Tally to say *yes ma'am*.

"Yes, ma'am," Tally sighed.

"I'll be home in just a little. Now, you go practice for Daddy."

"I will," Tally replied. "Ma'am."

"Love you. See you in a few."

"Love you, too."

There was a click as she hung up that resounded in the silence of the workroom.

At seven-forty-five she was putting on her coat. If that man thinks we will *ever* use his business again, so help me God, she thought. If he doesn't think I won't give him a piece of my mind… I will light into him so fast his damn head will spin. She stopped at the sound of wheels crunching onto the light snow in the driveway. The refracted shine of headlights spread over the windowpanes through the frosty glass.

She buttoned her coat and threw her muffler around her neck and stormed out.

"Are you Mr. Hunter?" she all but shouted, her teeth chattering from cold and rage. "I have been waiting here for *two and a half hours*," she slowed down for emphasis. "I have missed dinner, I have missed putting my child to bed and *you* didn't have the courtesy to call. You had *better* have a good explanation…"

"It's Mr. Walker. Where do you want these?" he asked icily.

"In there." She pointed toward the small shed by the door, standing her ground. "So…where were you and why are you late?"

"And," he continued. "Just so you know. There was a bad accident out by Hollin Hall. I was trying to help the emergency team. Traffic was backed up for six miles. Oh, and before I forget…I didn't notice any phones booths out on that road. So, if you will excuse me, Mrs. Marshall…."

He moved brusquely past her, slamming down the tailgate, pulling the heavy crates toward the edge of the bed of the truck.

"Oh." France didn't know what to say. She was embarrassed by her outburst. She stepped toward him.

"I am sorry. I don't know what to say," she said, chagrined. "That really isn't like me to fly off the handle like that. I had no idea…"

His face softened. "Apology accepted. It's late, we're all tired."

"Can I help carry these?"

"They're heavy," he stated, looking at her tiny frame.

"I'm stronger than I look," she said lightly, drawing herself up to her full height of five feet, two inches. "I grew up on a farm."

"You did? Whereabouts?"

"Outside Richmond. Henrico County."

"I know that area. What was the name of your farm?"

" 'Clifton.' "

"I've heard of it. Never been there, though. Here's one of the lighter boxes. That should help get you home faster."

They walked in silence, their breath steaming in the cold air.

When the last box was placed in the shed, Hunter turned to France.

"Anything else?"

She looked him in the dim light. Nice face, wavy, copper-colored hair, blue eyes. Tall, taller than Steve, with a rugged outdoorsiness to him.

"No, I think that about does it. Thank you. Hunter," she gently touched his sleeve as he turned.

"Yeah?"

"I am really sorry."

"Already forgotten." For the first time he smiled, a wide smile that lit up his face. "Tell Bernadette that she can sign off on these when I bring the rest of the order on Friday."

"I will. Thanks. Be careful."

"You, too. Go slow. There are some bad ice patches on the roads."

She watched him back his truck out and disappear into the night.

CHAPTER SIXTEEN

Christmas 1975

"I really don't feel like spending Christmas at your farm, France. Why can't we just spend it here? I'm probably going to have to fly out to California right after New Year's, anyway."

Steve and France were sitting at their kitchen table, across from each other. France was working lotion into her chapped, aching hands.

She narrowed her eyes at Steve. "Mama is not doing well, and you know it…"

"All the more reason not to burden her…"

"Stop and let me finish." France's words were strained. "Everyone will be there. You know good and darn well that we don't know how long we're going to have her. Your trip to California…" she stopped herself. The words *to see your slut* were right there, at the tip of her tongue. All she had to do was say them, to roll them off her tongue and out in the open, where all her suspicions and fears would find some kind of resolution, either through aggressive anger or stony silence. And she would know. But she couldn't bring herself to say it, to spit it out. She knew that, if she did, she would be forced to act. But now was not the time. Not with Mama so sick. Only one problem at a time. It was all she could handle.

"What about my trip to California?" Steve asked bluntly. France almost detected something challenging in the way he said it.

Steadily, she faced him. "Your trip to California cannot take precedence over the needs of the rest of my family right now." There. A little bit more time bought.

Steve looked away in frustration. "Okay, you win."

"It's not about winning. It's about family right now." You can't argue with that, you selfish ingrate, she thought. "Tally needs to be with Grannah as much as she can and she hasn't seen her in a few weeks."

Steve searched for a rebuttal. "Maybe it wouldn't be a good idea for Tally to see her so frail…"

"Steve. She needs to see my mother. We can go see your parents on the 23rd, spend the night, and head back on up to the farm."

Steve shrugged. "Okay. That's it. We go to Richmond."

"Steve, you can't deny that you haven't seen your family in an age. Come on."

He stood up, abruptly shoving his chair back. "Okay. I said we'd go."

She watched him exit the room, and she felt too tired to be hurt. It would be so nice if he would even pat her on the back and ask how she was doing. He had to know that she felt as though she would break from the worry. She felt so alone through all this. She was surprised by a sudden surge of anger that coursed through her. Her parents had been so good to him. They didn't deserve this. How dare he?

Driving down old State Road 17 to Tidewater, they wound through picturesque little towns like Tappahannock and Port Royal. Tucked into the back seat of the station wagon, Tally was in a frenzy of excitement. France actually felt sorry for the department store Santas that were accosted by the child. She would race up to them, pulling on their sleeves, demanding, "I want a baby doll and you need to bring it to 'Clifton' and not Virginia Beach *and don't forget.*" The poor souls would look at France in confusion. Even the hapless Salvation Army Santas came under fire.

"Look, Tally, see this creek? Can you read the sign? It says Peumansend Creek."

Tally looked up in interest.

"There was a very bad man named Peuman, who was a *pirate*," France went on. "The men who lived in this village...Port Royal...had about had enough of this pirate."

"What did they do to him?" Tally's eyes were wide.

"They chased him to the creek."

"Did they kill him?" Tally asked matter-of-factly.

"They did."

"Did they shoot him or stick him with their...what are those things?"

"Swords."

"Stick him with their swords?"

"I'm not sure, honey. But he met his end right there. That's why it's called Peuman's End Creek."

Tally chuckled. "Maybe that's why his name was Poo."

France tried to look stern but smiled. "Tally." Even Steve laughed.

The bridge tunnel came into view, stretching across the cold waters of the Chesapeake Bay. The dark shadows of the Navy ships were lined up in their berths across the bay. Some of them had Christmas lights strung on their railings, a flicker of cheer in the somber grayness. France always felt a twinge of sadness for the servicemen on those ships at this time of year, away from their homes and loved ones. Homesickness was tough.

It was almost nightfall when they pulled into the Marshall's driveway at Birdneck. White candles twinkled from every window and the colored lights of the Christmas tree shone from within.

The door opened.

"Come in! Hurry! It's cold!"

They embraced, standing in the hall, the smell of a good Smithfield ham wafting from the kitchen. Steve reacted to a well-aimed punch on the arm.

"What the…? Grady!" He turned to his parents. "You didn't warn me?" He was laughing.

"We wanted to surprise you!" Mrs. Marshall laughed with him.

Grady was at least an inch taller than Steve, in his third year at the Air force Academy. He hadn't been home in a year.

Grady hugged France and scooped up Tally.

"How's the little worm?"

Tally squealed. "Don't call me that!"

Steve and Grady went to the car to haul in luggage and Christmas presents. Tally was counting her presents under the tree.

"I have more than anyone!" she shouted.

As France lit the candles for dinner, she could hear Steve and Grady, punching each other and wrestling in the hall.

Mrs. Marshall shook her head and smiled. "Some things never change, do they?"

"No they don't. They remind me of Will and his friend. Boys are so physical."

"It's a different world, isn't it? I always wondered what having a daughter would be like…now I've got you and Tally."

"I would love to have a little boy…" she looked up quickly. "But that won't happen any time soon."

France could see the inchoate expression on Mrs. Marshall's face. News of another grandchild would have been well-received.

Dinner was wonderful, much quieter than 'Clifton', but so warm and pleasant.

France was extremely fond of her in-laws. They always made her feel so appreciated. After dessert everyone lingered at the table, basking in the comfortable surroundings.

Tally almost fell asleep with her head in her plate, so France gently carried her to her bed and tucked her in. She was surprised that Steve followed her in.

"Is the key to your parent's cottage still hidden behind that loose shingle?" he whispered.

She turned to face him. They were standing an inch apart, his breath warm on her cheek.

"It is," she whispered back.

"Mommy, I don't want to go to bed," whined Tally.

"I'll tell you what, darlin', "France said gently. "You have to go to bed, but you don't have to go to sleep, okay?"

"Okay, Mommy," Tally said drowsily. Her breath became even and regular.

"Let's go over there." Steve slid his hand around her waist.

"When?" There was something strangely exciting about this.

"Now. Let's tell my folks we need to go to the store…"

"Okay…"

They held hands running up the sandy pathway toward the cottage. The winter winds were whipping a tattered flag on a neighboring flagpole.

The cottage smelled beachy and musty and closed-up.

"It's freezing in here," France said, teeth chattering. Steve threw some logs into the fireplace, rubbing his hands briskly as he waited for a flame to catch.

France pulled some heavy quilts from the old blanket chest in the dining room. "They smell like mothballs, but they're warm," she smiled.

"Where's the wine?"

"It's in my bag," she said.

The liquid was warming as they sipped it, the reflections of the flames dancing off their stemmed glasses. They huddled close. Steve put his empty glass down and kissed her.

"This kind of feels good," he whispered, kissing her neck.

She finished her wine and kissed him. His intense response caught her off guard.

He pushed her back onto the quilts and they tore at each other's clothes and made love passionately. He held her tightly afterward.

"Wow," was all he managed to say.

There was a lot she wanted to say, but the pleasant sleepiness pervading her body made any thoughts she had drift away like sand in an incoming tide.

Steve checked his watch. "Damn," he said. "We need to get back. How are we going to explain spending this much time at the store?" He leaned in and kissed her.

"I love you, France."

"I love you, too." In that moment, she meant it. Had he?

The next morning Steve loaded up the car for the trip to 'Clifton'. His family lined up at the door to say goodbye.

France hugged her mother-in-law.

"'Bye, Mom. Merry Christmas. We'll call you when we get back to Alexandria."

"France…" the older woman pulled back.

France felt her cheeks flush. She felt oddly guilty about the previous night, like a teenager caught misbehaving in the back seat of a car. She raised her eyebrows in expectation.

"Clay and I were happy to see you and Steve doing so well."

France realized that her own parents were not the only people in the world worried about them.

"We are, Mom. We are doing better. We've had our ups and downs, of course…but I think we're going to be okay."

"Good, dear. That's what we want to hear." She smiled broadly and kissed her on the cheek.

"Merry Christmas."

In the car, France rubbed the foggy window, catching a glimpse of the family clustered at the door, waving goodbye.

It was late afternoon when the Richmond skyline came into view. A dusting of light snow powdered the rooftops. A few tall buildings scraped the sky, and the unique dome of the Medical College of Virginia was silhouetted in the distance.

"Did I ever tell you that I was almost engaged to a boy who just graduated from MCV?" she asked.

"No, I don't think you did. " Steve glanced at her briefly, trying to keep his focus on the traffic going into the city.

"We dated on and off through high school. Our parents were friends. I kind of forgot about him that summer I met you."

Steve laughed. "I guess like heck you did." He patted her hand.

She looked back at Tally in the back seat, pressing her nose against the window. I wonder what my life would be like if I hadn't met Steve? she mused.

The city thinned into suburbs and then into countryside.

"I see the cedar trees! And the stables!" cried out Tally excitedly.

They turned up the long drive leading up to the main house. Two boxwood wreaths were hung on the large double front doors. Tally couldn't get out of the car fast enough.

"Tally!" said Steve sternly. "Wait until I've parked the car!"

She was already out and running up the steps.

The door opened and they all spilled into the warm hallway. France stood drinking it all in. Pine rope wound its way up the banister; in the dining room she could see the cone of apples and lemon and sprigs of boxwood, topped by a pineapple. Magnolia leaves fanned out at the base.

Her father was greeting everyone.

"Where's Grannah?" shouted Tally.

"She's waiting for you all in the kitchen" he answered gently. "There are lots of surprises this time of year," he smiled, looking at France.

"Daddy, how did you pull this off?" she asked, pointing to the greenery.

"It's Christmas…" he said simply.

"Daddy, making all that stuff is a lot of work." She held up her hands for him to see. "My hands are *raw* from making all that stuff for Bernadette. *You* haven't made a wreath a day in your life."

"Surprise!" Martha jumped up from her seat at the kitchen table.

"Oh, my Lord!" France gasped. "I thought you all weren't coming in until ten tonight."

"I came in a few days early," she said quietly. "Somebody had to get the house ready. And Daddy is hopeless."

"I am so glad to see you…Mama, how are you? You look *great*." France tried to control the sharp intake of air that was her response to seeing her mother. She was shocked at how weak Mama looked. Her fine, chiseled features stood out in contrast to the papery, sallow skin stretched across her lovely, aristocratic face. A heavy shawl was pulled around her thin shoulders. Daddy had warned her that Mama was cold all the time. But her eyes were bright and her smile was genuine.

"So glad to see *you*, honey."

Tally was draped on one arm.

"Tally, honey, don't lean on Grannah."

"She's just fine, darlin'," her mother returned, patting Tally's shoulder with her free hand. "I'm so glad my little Tally is here."

"So…when will Richard and the boys get here?" she asked, turning to her sister.

"They should get here by supper."

"Where's Will?"

"He's on his way. He went to pick up his girlfriend at the airport."

"Will has a girlfriend who needs to be picked up at the airport? When did this happen? I thought he was seeing that little girl…what was her name? Dabney."

"He was… but Sylvie was a French exchange student. She went home a few weeks ago, but is flying in to have Christmas with us."

"And her parents are okay with this?"

Martha shrugged. "I guess so. They think it's educational. Besides, she's French. She's eighteen, and pretty sophisticated, from what Mama says."

"Why didn't anybody tell me? I am always out of the loop."

154

"Well, for one thing, this all just came about in the last few days. And, secondly, it's not like you ever pick up your phone. I've tried to call you about twenty times."

France looked sheepish. "I'm sorry, you're right. I haven't called anyone. I try to call Mama when I can, but she's not much up for talking."

"Understandably. She's been right sick. I think she's doing incredibly well, considering."

"I'm not sure. I hope she is. I wasn't prepared for her to look this bad this quickly." France sighed deeply. "I have been working my patootie off. It's Christmas. Everyone wants a wreath. I'm exhausted."

The kitchen was glowing and warm. A fire roared in the fireplace and the smell of Mama's hot apple cider permeated the entire house.

France and Martha settled in a chair on either side of their mother. She smiled and placed her hands on each of theirs.

"My girls," she said.

France sipped her mug of cider. "The best in the world," she breathed happily.

"Always put a little orange juice and cinnamon in it," Mama said. "It cuts the sweetness."

Dinner was in the dining room, promptly at seven, as always. Candles were lit twinkling from hurricanes on the mantel, and the table groaned under the weight of Smithfield ham, succulent Lynnhaven oysters that were sent up as a Christmas present from Steve's parents, yeast rolls, cranberry salad, sweet potatoes, and green beans. Christmas pudding followed for dessert and Tally and her cousins, Taylor and Mosby, enjoyed hot chocolate while the adults had plantation eggnog. France knew how much work went into that eggnog; farm eggs beaten to a froth, Kentucky bourbon, and fresh cream and hand-grated cinnamon. That old Talbot recipe was to be savored, never swigged.

France caught Steve looking at her from across the table. What an odd expression he was wearing, she thought. Even though he winked when she met his gaze, she was troubled. The room was filled with the din of fifteen people all seemingly talking at once. She liked Sylvie, the little French girl. She was very pretty and stylish in that French way; Will was clearly besotted with her. Martha was leaning in toward her husband Richard, sharing a secret little joke. They had a great relationship, realized France. Her eyes traveled around the table; Aunt Scott and Uncle Embry, Aunt Janis and Uncle Sonny. Her cousins lived too far away to come; several of them were living in Boston. Her mother was enlivened by the gathering and was talking animatedly. Color was back in her face. France almost forgot, just for a little minute, that Mama was sick. Everyone made toasts.

At ten, everyone started clearing the tables and making ready to drive to the midnight service at St. John's in Richmond.

"I want to see the Christmas tree!" shouted Tally on the way to the car, her shrill voice echoing in the still night air.

"Not until tomorrow morning," said France firmly. "You know we never see the tree until Christmas morning."

"Can I say the "D" word?" Tally asked innocently.

France saw her father arch his brows ever so slightly.

"No you may not. And how do you know about the "D" word anyway, little missy?"

"Daddy says it when he's mad. Why does he get to say it and not me?"

"When you get to be Daddy's age, I'll let you say it...sometimes., but not until then. Way to go, Steve," she hissed under her breath.

He shrugged. "I didn't know she heard me."

The old plaster walls of the church glowed in the candlelight. It was a sung service with communion and carols accompanied by trumpets and timpani. The music swelled to the rafters, and France's heart swelled with it. Tally was nestled on her grandfather's lap, his leathery hand stroking the child's smooth cheek. She smiled looking at the two of them. Some images are forever burned into memory; she felt sure that this would be one of them.

They all said goodbye outside the church as the aunts and uncles headed back to their houses in the Fan and Church Hill in the city. France noticed how strong the Richmond accents of the old guard were. She thought her own was strong enough, but it was definitely a watered-down version of theirs.

The moon glistened on what was left of the snow, which crunched underfoot as they made it back to 'Clifton'. Steve and Daddy were helping Mama up to the house, and France and Martha and Richard were sprinting ahead to keep up with the children.

"They're going to open that parlor door, sure as the world," Martha panted.

"Tally!" France called.

Tally turned. "Yes, mommy?"

"You are not to open the parlor door, do you hear?"

She saw Tally whisper something to Taylor and Mosby.

"Yes ma'am," she said.

"Now go get your pajamas on so you can hang your stockings on the kitchen fireplace and get to bed. You don't want to be awake when St. Nicholas comes."

"He'll come here first," Tally told the twins importantly. They nodded.

"Lord, she's bossy. Your boys are doing everything she tells them to do. They need to stand up to her."

"It's a seniority thing. I did that to you when we were little."

By the time the children were finally asleep, they slipped downstairs. Presents were stacked underneath the tree and Richard and Steve were putting together a doll carriage.

"Did I hear the "D" word fly out of your mouth?" France asked, kneeling beside Steve.

"Probably," he acknowledged. "This thing is complicated, and I'm good at assembly."

She moved toward Daddy in his wing chair next to the fireplace.

"Is that the tree, Daddy?" France whispered.

Years ago France and her father had come across the perfect cedar when looking for a Christmas tree. It was by the pond in their woods.

"It is," smiled her father.

"I really wanted to cut it down that day, but you wouldn't let me. Why?"

"Because it needed a little more size on it...and it was so perfect, that I wanted to save it for just the right time."

She didn't say anything more. He was right. This Christmas, for all of them, would be perfect. Perfect, and fragile and beautiful, like the ancient glass-blown ornaments shining from the boughs on the perfect cedar tree.

CHAPTER SEVENTEEN

February 1976

The rain outside the shop window slowed to a cold drizzle. As she watched the droplets stream down the windows, France thought what a difficult month February could be. It was no accident that Valentine's Day fell in the middle of it. Everyone needed the punch of red hearts to pierce the gray bleakness of the month. It was the only thing that could lift the spirits.

She was restless and distracted. Her instincts were telling her she should be worried about something, but what? Tally was at school; Mama appeared to be doing a little bit better.

There was a tiny improvement in her relationship with Steve since Christmas, although it hadn't kept him from flying out to California three times since then, she thought ruefully.

Someday, someday, she thought, I am just going to have to have it out with that boy.

But confrontation took energy. Between getting Tally straight at school and the holidays that seemed to be seamlessly running together in her work at Bernadette's, she was just too damned tired. It was weird how things worked in a marriage. Every tiny improvement was like throwing a scrap of food to a hungry dog. It was sustaining. She even felt lulled into thinking things were good. Not great, but very good. Okay, she could take that, for now.

Two-thirty. She pushed aside the arrangement she had been working on and stretched her neck. She needed to finish it. She was up to her elbows in flower arrangements and work orders and her hands and back ached with the close work.

Where was Hunter? He was due any minute with a fresh load of ivy and smilax. She smiled inwardly thinking of him. After their rough start they had developed a decent working relationship. He was engaging, with his quick wit and easy way. He always found something nice to say. She could be wearing the rattiest flannel shirt and muddy Wellingtons and rusty jeans and she would feel beautiful when he was gone. How did he do it? She wished he were already here; his cheerful presence would push her forebodings out the window.

She felt the need to just do something, so she went over to the phone and dialed her parent's number.

"Ridley's."

"Hey, Mama."

"Hi, darlin'! What a surprise! Is everything okay?" Her voice sounded slightly anxious.

"Can't a girl ever call home without there being an emergency? I'm just a little homesick, that's all."

"Can you come down any time soon?"

"Not until after Valentine's Day. It's almost the busiest time for us."

"How's Tally?"

"Growing like a little weed. I swear, she's put on three inches since December."

Her mother laughed. "Well, you need to get that child over here while I can still get her on my lap."

"I will. I thought about coming the weekend after Valentine's... I've put in so many hours that I will need a break. Steve will be going to California that week, anyway."

"I see." Her mother was quiet for a minute, but brightened. "Well, it would be perfect to come down then. Could you come early? Maybe Friday?"

"I can't, Mama. I promised Tally that I would take her and her friend Jenna to the movies to see Star Wars."

"Well, all right."

"But we'll leave first thing in the morning on Saturday, I promise."

"Well, we can't wait to see you. You know that."

"I know, Mama. How are you?"

"Much, much better. I put on three pounds this week."

The relief in France's voice was apparent. "That's great. How about Daddy? Is he around today?"

"No, he decided to go into the office today, even though he said he wasn't feeling well."

"What did he say was wrong?"

"I don't think it's anything to worry about. I think he's just tired, that's all. He wore himself out hauling firewood up to the house yesterday."

"Why didn't he let Jamerson do it?" France knew why, but asked anyway. Jamerson probably hadn't shown up.

"Well, honey, Jamerson called in sick yesterday…"

At least he called in, thought France. That had to be a first.

"…and Daddy knew we were getting low…"

"Daddy shouldn't be pushing himself."

"Well, you might as well tell him not to breathe. You know Daddy."

"Oh, Mama. " France could hear truck tires in the drive. "I'm going to have to run. The delivery guy is here."

"All right."

I love you, Mama."

"I love you, too, precious."

She saw Hunter wheeling a dolly loaded with greenery up the misty walk. His red muffler stood out in contrast to the pewter sky.

"Hey, there, good-lookin'," he smiled as he coaxed the dolly through the door.

"Hey to you," she smiled back.

His skin was ruddy with the cold and droplets of rain clung to his copper hair.

"I knew there was a reason to come out in this mess."

"That's nice, Hunter. That's a really *nice* thing to say. Thank you." She felt her cheeks burn. "I was kind of hoping I'd be worth a trip out in the rain to someone."

"Everything okay?"

"Yeah…I was just on the phone with Mama."

"How is she?" His concern was genuine.

"Better, really. She's starting to put on some weight. She said Daddy isn't feeling well, though."

"I'm sorry to hear that. What's the matter with him?"

"I don't know." She felt the old anxiety start to swell within her again. "That worthless Jamerson- he's the guy who's supposed to help out on the farm- called in sick and Daddy just had to go haul a bunch of firewood up to the house.,. and... you know the rest."

"Is he in bed?"

France snorted. "Are you kidding? He should be, but not Daddy. No, he went in to work this morning."

"That's a tough generation," Hunter said reflectively. "We should all be so tough."

She nodded. "In all my born days I can't remember him staying home for any reason, sick, healthy, or otherwise. I guess it's kept him young."

"My old man was the same way. He passed away two years ago. He went out to the barn to feed the horses, and didn't come back in. We went looking for him..."

A shadow passed over his face.

"Oh, Hunter. I'm so sorry."

"He lived a good life and died doing what he loved. What he knew... Not too many people can ask for better than that."

France nodded. Her eyes rested on the clock.

"Do you need to be somewhere?"

"I need to pick up Tally from school. But I can't leave until Bee gets here..."

"Where does she go to school?"

"Gunstan Hall Elementary."

"The traffic wasn't too bad when I came in. It shouldn't take long to get there. How old is she now?"

"Almost seven."

"Does she look like you?"

"If you put our baby pictures side-by-side, you couldn't tell us apart. Everyone says she's me made over."

"She must be a beauty then."

"Thanks, Hunter." She couldn't bring herself to meet his gaze.

In the years to come, the memory of that moment would be etched in France's brain forever. The way the lamplight lit up the top of Hunter's hair, the deep lines around his eyes when he smiled. She remembered the cool edge of the metal-rimmed table under her fingertips. The sharp jangle of the telephone ringing, piercing the air, and the way she jumped at the sound of it. The cool Bakelite finish of the black phone as she picked up the heavy receiver to answer it.

"Bernadette's." It was so normal. She had answered it so *normally.* "I'm sorry, can you speak up? I can't hear you…"

She even remembered smiling up at Hunter as she shook her head, indicating that she had no idea who was on the other end of the line.

"France, it's Mama." Her mother's voice was strangled. "It's Daddy, honey," she said brokenly.

"Daddy?" Daddy's at the office, she remembered thinking. She felt so calm. He went to work this morning, even though he wasn't feeling well. Just like always.

"Honey, he's gone. He died about thirty minutes ago. They think it was his heart."

The week was a blur. So much to do. 'Clifton' had a steady stream of relatives and well-wishers constantly coming through the door. Food had to be laid out, and there was so much food. Everyone sent it. She and Martha both did double duty, greeting visitors and replenishing the food. Not to mention standing watch over Mama, who was holding up.

They marveled at her strength.

"It's all that good breeding," Martha whispered during a lull to France.

France herself was thankful that it had been passed down to them. It kept them smiling when they didn't feel like they would ever smile again. It kept them solicitous, always making sure their guests were looked after, even as their bodies were screaming that they were the ones that needed looking after.

"Look at her," whispered France. They were in the dining room, watching their mother engage in a conversation with a distant family member.

"She looks radiant," whispered Martha back.

"Well, we're going to be burying her next if she doesn't slow down."

Martha was shocked. "Don't you even say that!"

"I'm sorry. I am just ready for everyone to leave us alone."

Martha put her hand on France's shoulder. "We're all tired. But we have to carry on. That's the way Daddy would have wanted it."

"No, Martha. I think that's the way Daddy would have expected it."

Martha looked at her thoughtfully. "And Mama."

"And Mama. They were both cut out of the same cloth."

The black hole yawned in front of the group clustered under black umbrellas in the light rain. Mama sat stoically under the little canopy that had been set up, flanked by France and Martha. For some reason, for France, seeing her brother Will trying to fight back tears was the saddest part of the day. He was trying so hard to be strong. Her heart went out to him.

She would always remember the shades of gray and all the black; the gray mist, the gray rain, the black clothes, the black hearse, the black, gaping hole of the grave. And the red, red punch of roses in the middle of all that misty gray and black.

CHAPTER EIGHTEEN

April 1976

It was always the same, the drive to 'Clifton'. The approach through autumn trees, with that strange diffusion of light, pink and silver. She could feel the car slide ever so slightly at the sharp turn. She would park at the gates and look up at the long drive shrouded in mist and heavy fog. Although she couldn't make out the house in the mist, she knew it was there, waiting for her. Her heart would quicken as she approached. The fog would never lift until she got to the first step and she would see it. The house was standing empty and dark, the front door always open, leading to emptiness.

She would put her hand on the door frame, willing herself to go in, but all she could do was call her father and hear the thin sound bounce and echo off the empty walls.

That was when she would wake up.

She sat alone at her kitchen table, nursing a cold cup of coffee. She wished she hadn't dropped Tally off at 'Clifton' yesterday, but Martha and the twins were staying the weekend there to be with Mama. Tally thrived on the farm and loved her cousins.

She and Martha had initially been worried that Mama would follow Daddy right quick, but she didn't. She was amazingly resilient, growing stronger every day.

It's me, thought France. *I'm* not dealing with it. Steve was in California *again*. As often as not when she would awake from these dreams, she found his side of the bed cold and empty. She wanted to feel some kind of reassuring human warmth, but it didn't come from him.

She did try to talk to him about it.

"Steve, I just feel so sad…I miss him so much. He was such a presence, wasn't he?" She could feel tears stinging behind her eyes.

Steve was short with her. "He was a great guy, France, but you need to snap out of it. Life goes on. So deal."

She sighed from deep within. "Can you delay your trip to California just a few days? Please?"

"Do you want food on your table? It's work, France. Work."

"I know. But I need you to be here with me. Please." She looked at him imploringly. "I won't ask again."

"If I give into you this time, you'll expect it. Besides," he nudged her shoulder, "you and Martha are your mother's daughters. You're both as tough as they come. C'mon, France. Do your mother proud. You don't need me around to coddle you."

She looked at him dully and said nothing as he packed his bags.

He pecked her on her forehead.

"I'll be back Monday. If I can get a flight on Sunday, I will. How's that?"

On this wet Saturday morning, the irony of spring wasn't lost on her. As she drove past a farm on her way to Bernadette's, she could see horses in foal, and the first spring lambs frolicking in the fields. The spiky branches of bright yellow forsythia along the fencerows brought the first color to the landscape and the redbud was promising to burst into bloom among the stands of trees, with bright new spring green leaves mixed in with the old.

She was the first one in the shop. It was still bitter and raw outside and she was already regretting the thin jacket she wore. She started a fire in the wood stove and stood beside it, waiting for warmth to start emanating into the room. She pulled a chair over to sit next to it. She leaned over and flipped on the radio, hoping that music would chase away the emptiness.

The harsh voice of the deejay stabbed the silence. "And let's take a walk down memory lane with a hit from the '60's…"

"*If you leave me now…*" spilled into the room.

France started to cry. She hadn't really cried for such a long time, not even when Daddy died. She couldn't. The tears were there, but they didn't come.

Suddenly, she was that long ago girl, teetering on the brink of a future sparkling with a thousand bright possibilities, dancing under a starry summer sky with a boy- a man- who would change her life forever. She sobbed huge, wracking sobs. Every time she thought it would stop, a fresh wave of grief and sadness washed over her and she cried some more.

She didn't hear anyone enter, and she jumped when she felt a hand on her shoulder.

"Hunter, I didn't hear you come in," she said, her voice raspy with grief. She jumped to her feet, desperately wiping away her tears.

"Are you all right?"

She nodded yes, but her face contorted with sorrow and she shook her head no.

He pulled her toward him, holding her tightly in his big, strong embrace. He smelled woodsy, the way

Daddy and Will used to smell when they came in from a day of hunting. His flannel shirt was rough against her face.

He said nothing, just held her until her body started to relax and she pulled back, her eyes swollen.

"For what?" he asked, incredulously. "Because you're missing your father? Because you're exhausted from carrying a heavy load? No need to apologize to anyone, France, least of all to me."

She bit her lip, hardly daring to look at him.

"Here, sit down," he said gently, awkwardly steering her back to her chair by the stove. "Let me get you something to drink." He looked around for the coffee maker.

"Over there," France pointed to a cabinet next to the desk. She heard him filling the carafe with water as the machine sputtered to life.

He pulled up a chair and brought over two steaming mugs of fresh coffee.

"I hope you like cream and sugar," he offered.

"Couldn't be better," she smiled, taking hers. She couldn't bring herself to tell him that she only took cream.

"Okay, okay," he spoke quietly. "A good cup of coffee always makes the world look better."

She nodded in agreement.

"Do you need me to call Bernadette?"

"No," she said quickly.

"What time is she due to get in?"

"In about half an hour."

"Where's your husband?"

"California."

His mouth became a grim, hard line. What kind of man would leave his wife when she was this vulnerable? He hardly knew France and could see how fragile she was.

"I think you need to go home," he said, suddenly.

"I can't," she protested. "It's almost Easter, and we've got all these corsages and arrangements to make..." her voice trailed off.

"I think Bernadette can do without you for one Saturday."

"She can't...really."

"She can. Trust me. Besides, she's been worried about you."

"She has?" France's bewilderment was genuine.

"Yes, she has. We all have. People care about you, France."

"Really? Thank you, Hunter. I...sort of needed to hear that today."

"You'd never know it, but Bernadette is an old mother hen, for all her ways."

"I guess I haven't worked here long enough to see that side of her."

"Well, she is. All she has to do is walk in here and see you looking like this," he reached out and tweaked her chin. "And she would be telling you to go home. You look terrible."

"Thanks a lot," France pulled back, turning away. She wished she had a mirror.

"The woman has a heart of gold," he continued. "For a damn Yankee."

"Okay," she said resignedly. "I'll go. You've convinced me. Wouldn't want to scare away the customers with how bad I look."

"Good girl," he slapped his knee. "I'll even follow you home, to make sure you get there okay."

"You really don't need to do that. I'll be fine. I can take care of myself."

"I won't stay. But I'd like to get you situated."

She frowned slightly. "Okay then. Follow me home.'

Driving home, she looked in her rear view mirror at the reassuring shine of Hunter's headlights behind her. She caught a glimpse of her reflection. Hunter was right. She looked terrible.

When she parked in her driveway, he clambered out of his truck behind her.

"Just making sure," was all he offered.

She turned to him. "You can stay a few minutes, if you'd like."

"It would be better if I didn't. I've got some Saturday deliveries to make."

She started to turn to go in, but felt that she couldn't.

"Hunter," she said. "If you could stay for just a little while, I would feel better. I don't really want to be by myself. Not right now."

He stood for a second and studied her face.

"Okay," he said slowly. "Let me borrow your phone when we get in, okay?"

"Of course," she nodded, and smiled.

She was sitting on the couch when he joined her in the living room.

"Nice house," he commented.

"Thanks. We like it."

He sat in the chair next to her.

"Aren't you glad you came home? You look better already."

"I am. Thanks. Sometimes it's kind of nice to have someone do the thinking for you."

"I wouldn't know." It was true. He'd never had that luxury. Didn't want it, really.

"I don't mean to get personal, France…stop me if you don't want to talk about it…"

What?"

"Why isn't your husband here?"

"He travels…a lot." Even she didn't buy that explanation.

"Okay, let me re-phrase the question. Why isn't he here?"

She shifted uncomfortably. "He just isn't, Hunter. There's really nothing to say about it."

He sat in silence, looking at his hands clasped between his knees.

"If you don't want to talk about it, it's okay," he finally said.

"I wouldn't even know where to start."

"Start at the beginning."

"Are you sure you want to hear it?"

He nodded.

She inhaled deeply. She wasn't good at this whole unloading business. Why did he want to know all this stuff about her anyway?

"It started on the beach, when I was just out of high school," she began. And the whole story spilled out from there. Once the floodgates opened, there was no stopping.

"Wow," he said when she reached a stopping point. "I have to ask you… are you happy? Have you had any good times?"

Laid out bare, her marriage looked pretty bad. She never realized…or, maybe, she never allowed herself to realize…

She stopped and thought. "Christmas. Christmas was actually a good time. We did have a great Christmas." Sadness washed over her as she thought of her father.

Seeing the shift in her expression, Hunter reached out and took her hand. "I'm sorry. I shouldn't have made you talk about it."

"No, it's okay. I think it's supposed to be good to talk about it. It's cathartic. I can't believe I actually burdened you with all of that. I am so sorry!" She frowned slightly. "Why *did* you want to talk about it? You don't really know me. I mean," she said quickly, "I appreciate you caring enough to ask, don't get me wrong."

Hunter half-smiled. "I don't know. I guess I just wondered, that's all. You talk about Tally, your family, but you hardly ever mention your husband. And…" he continued, "you don't look happy."

"I don't?" Wow, she thought. I always thought that I did.

"No, you don't. I mean, you smile and act cheerful. But I get the feeling that's you. I think you would act that way if the world was caving in."

France smiled ironically. "That's a Talbot thing…Mama's side," she explained. "We were raised to square off and face the world. No matter what."

"I guess that's what I like about you. Not many people can do that these days."

She closed her eyes. "I wouldn't know about that," she said simply.

"Have you tried counseling?"

"No, not really. I guess we should. But I went to California to a wedding last fall at Mama's urging…kind of a last ditch effort to get some quality time…"

"And?"

"And it was a complete wash. A disaster. I was even paranoid about him talking to the maid of honor. I mean, I didn't even like being around me! That's why I was surprised- pleasantly, I might add- that we actually got along at Christmas. I didn't know where we were going. But I had Mama to worry about. I back-burnered my marriage."

"What are you going to do?"

"I don't know. Take it a day at a time, I expect. That's about all I can do, right now."

"I admire you, France. I admire your strength."

"Thanks. For all the good it does me. I appreciate the shoul…"

She stopped at the sound of a key turning in the door.

"Steve?"

Steve dropped his bags in the hall, stepping over his briefcase.

She half-stood. Hunter got to his feet and extended his hand.

"What the f....?" Steve's face was livid. His face was florid, and his lips were white.

"No, no, no, Steve," France said desperately. "I wasn't feeling well and Hunter followed me home to make sure I was okay, that's all." She looked from one man to the other.

Hunter withdrew his hand, his own face a picture of rage. He raised his eyebrows and looked at France.

She nodded her head quickly. "It's okay, go."

"Are you sure?" he asked.

"I'm sure, I'm sure, just go." Her voice was urgent.

He picked his way past the sofa, his eyes never leaving Steve. They heard the door close quietly behind him.

"There was no real reason for me to hurry back, was there?" The hard, cold tone of his voice made her shiver.

She stood with her hand on the back of the chair. Her red-hot rage burned white and turned her into ice.

"So this is what happens when I'm away on business, trying to earn enough money to give you a nice damn life."

She said nothing, but her eyes bored through him, through his red face, his white lips, into his heart.

"You have nothing to say? No rebuttal? No apologies? No freaking excuse? Instead you bring some friggin' hired hand into the friggin' house I've about killed myself to provide for you and God knows what you've been doing behind my back? You're a stupid whore."

She inhaled twice. Her words were measured, steely. "How. Dare. You. How *dare* you accuse me of anything? Coming from the guy who couldn't even keep his pants up during the birth of his child…"

Steve started to say something and stopped.

Her anger fueled her strength. "From the guy who runs to the west coast every other day under the *guise* of earning money for *me*? I have *never* done the first thing to betray you. Never. Do you hear me? Never. Now, let me hear you tell me the same thing. You go right ahead."

Steve stared at her.

"I don't think I need to explain myself to you." He tried to draw himself up intimidatingly.

"There's where you're wrong."

He glared at her.

"You have two damn seconds."

His mouth was hard.

"Time's up," she said. "You can't. Get your cheating, bottom-feeding ass out of *my* house. Now."

Steve threw his head back defiantly. "You can't throw me out of my house. And what about Tally?"

"What about her? You've had plenty of time to think about Tally on all your trips. It didn't stop you from going, did it?"

"You can't kick me out of the house, France." He suddenly sounded a little less sure, a little less defiant. His voice even sounded like he was pleading.

"There's where you're wrong again. I can, and I am. I am kicking you out. So get out. Now. Oh, and Steve," she added. "Just so you know. I will be able to prove everything."

The statement hung like an ominous cloud between them. He stepped toward her. His impulse was to grab her, hug her, hold her. But she recoiled from him.

"I said, get out."

He turned, yanking his bags with him, and closed the door.

France heard the car start and peel out of the driveway, pulling the tattered remnants of their marriage behind it, like so many cans tied to the bumper of a car on a wedding day.

There was no looking back.

CHAPTER NINETEEN

Virginia Beach, Virginia
1990

Steve stood at the back of the church with Tally fluttering next to him like a small bird. He scanned the sanctuary, allowing his eyes to rest on the few familiar faces he could pick out of the crowd. There were his parents, his mother beaming from her seat at the front, his father stooped and quiet.

Grady sat next to them, looking tired and beleaguered. He'd left his wife, now pregnant with twins, up in Boston and had flown down to be there for the occasion. He gave Steve a thumb's up when he saw him. Steve nodded. He wished Charlie could be there. He could have used his wit to alleviate some of the tension.

France's side of the church was packed, but then, she came from a huge family. Conspicuously missing were her parents; Mrs. Ridley had been gone about five years, or so he had heard.

The organ started to play *Purcell's Trumpet Voluntary in D* and he could feel Tally stiffen as she dug her fingers into his arm.

"Show time, " he whispered, trying to smile reassuringly at his wide-eyed daughter.

Good God, she looks like her mother, he thought as they started up the aisle. The resemblance was so strong it was uncanny. He had the surreal feeling that he was the groom, watching a young France make her way up the same aisle.

He could see France in the front, wearing a short dress in a becoming shade of periwinkle. She has aged really well, he had to admit. Her hair was still dark and her face unlined, even after all those summers on the beach. She was trim and had an aura of success about her. Apparently she owned her own landscape design company and Tally mentioned that she was living at Ridley Cottage with Hunter Walker. His jaw clenched at the thought. Where was he, he wondered. France was clearly by herself. Martha was there, and Rich. He could see the twins. It looked like the whole clan had made it.

At the altar he released Tally's hand with a little squeeze and caught her gaze. He felt a brief pang of regret. They were not close. It surprised him that she asked him to give her away. Her expression was unreadable.

He looked at Scott and felt a sense of satisfaction with her choice. He was ambitious and had focus. And it was apparent he loved Tally.

Leaning in, he kissed Tally's cheek, put her hand in Scott's and patted Scott's arm before taking his seat. He looked over at France, who was glowing with pride. Their eyes met and, for one brief instant, all the years of history combined into one palpable moment. He pulled his gaze from France and his eyes met Lana's, sitting on the bench with his empty spot awaiting him. He knew she was wondering if he was remembering his wedding day here so many years ago. He tried to look encouraging. The years had sucked all color and vibrancy from Lana. She was so faded she was almost monochromatic.

He moved in next to her and put his arm around her. Sunlight was filtering through the old windows, diffusing the walls to gold. The little chapel had weathered twenty-two summers since he'd been there last, but really hadn't changed all that much, except for the hollow sounds of heavy traffic outside the walls.

So here he was. The full circle. Chapter opened, chapter closed. His daughter was launched, embarking on her own journey.

Seeing the tiny girl in white whispering her vows to the tall man standing next to her, Steve wondered what life might have been like if he hadn't missed everything. If he hadn't walked away from France and Tally and that life with them, to board the first available flight out, to California and to a waiting Lana.

EPILOGUE

Stretching languorously, France looked at her watch. She knew Hunter would be firing up the grill, but she still didn't feel ready to remove herself from the beach. She loved the beach at dusk. She could reclaim this small, sandy stretch as her own, where life made sense, and all conflict, indecision and the vagaries of circumstance were reduced to the insignificance of shadows playing on the waves.

She frowned. Why hadn't she wanted Hunter to attend the wedding this afternoon? He had accepted her decision, probably chalking it up to the potential awkwardness of the occasion, but that wasn't really it. She wasn't sure she really understood it herself. Most of the time she wanted his strong presence by her side, to bolster and support her through times that she anticipated would be difficult. But today was different. Maybe she just wanted some kind of closure with Steve and Tally, for it to be just the three of them, one last time. But Lana was there, so what difference did it make? It just did.

She felt a surge of warmth thinking about Hunter. She knew he wanted to marry her, but was wise enough not to press her. It wasn't that she didn't love him; she did love him, with all her heart. His strength, his honor, his goodness of heart. He shielded her from so much. When she was with him, all bad and sad things seemed worlds away. He and Daddy were the standard by which she judged all men.

Still, she couldn't relinquish the freedom that came with being on her own. For all accounts and purposes they might as well be married. Maybe some day....

Part of her wanted to stay on the beach until nightfall. Long ago she felt afraid to be on the beach after dark, even the familiar beach she had known all her life. The vast expanse of black sea and sky used to make her feel small and vulnerable. Now it felt like a warm velvet cloak, something that she could draw around her and be enveloped by.

She realized she was tired to the bone; weddings were grueling, emotional roller coasters. She was glad it was behind her now, although it meant closing the door on a large segment of her life, saying good-bye to her only child. Tally was so young, yet she was almost four years older than France was on her wedding day.

All those memories, flooding back into her mind, heart and spirit. Usually locked away, until the odd time that a song, a film, or a photograph would call the memory back up. That was about the only time she really ever thought of Steve. He was there in the crazy quilt of her youth, and would float to the surface as a flicker of recognition toward a distant acquaintance of long ago, as amorphous as the shape of a sand castle being erased by the tide, leaving the beach a blank slate, ready for the sand castles of tomorrow.